Tyler Anne Snell genuinely loves all genres of the written word. However, she's realized that she loves books filled with sexual tension and mysteries a little more than the rest. Her stories have a good dose of both. Tyler lives in Alabama with her same-named husband and their mini "lions." When she isn't reading or writing, she's playing video games and working on her blog, *Almost There*. To follow her shenanigans, visit tylerannesnell.com.

Loving Baby

TYLER ANNE SNELL

MILLS & BOON

First published in Great Britain 2018
by Mills & Boon, an imprint of HarperCollins*Publishers*
1 London Bridge Street, London, SE1 9GF

Large Print edition 2018

© 2018 Tyler Anne Snell

ISBN: 978-0-263-07767-4

MIX
Paper from
responsible sources
FSC™ C007454

This book is produced from independently certified
FSC™ paper to ensure responsible forest management.
For more information visit www.harpercollins.co.uk/green.

Printed and bound in Great Britain
by CPI Group (UK) Ltd, Croydon, CR0 4YY

This book is for Holli Anne. I've been waiting for a heroine that I thought you'd be proud of, and I think Suzy is it! She's an awesome mom, an amazing person and is stronger than even she knows. Basically a rock-star human, like you! Thank you for being my beautiful, rule-breaking moth and also the best Anne out there. Love you to the moon and back, Perkins/Knope!

Prologue

"Well, this isn't good."

Suzanne Simmons looked down at the body with a growing sense of dread. It wasn't strong enough to scatter her thoughts or turn her stomach cold, but it did warrant a worried glance at Detective Matt Walker, standing next to her. His face was hard, his eyes sharp as they scanned the dead man at their feet. He crouched down.

"No, this isn't good at all," he agreed. "Not if that's Gardner Todd."

They lapsed into thoughtful silence as each did their own private inspection of the man without touching him. He was in his mid-thirties, white and dressed in work coveralls. His boots were new but dirty, with maybe a few weeks' use. He had a tattoo peeking out at his wrist, a silver ring on his right index finger and three bullets in his belly.

But if it *was* Gardner Todd, then his death was the least of their worries.

"I guess that, for once, our department of front porch justice got it right," Matt said after a moment. "Our caller *did* hear gunshots and not a car backfiring."

The detective was referring to the older woman named June who had called in to the Riker County Sheriff's Department, swearing up and down she'd heard a gunfight at the abandoned warehouse two blocks over from her house. Both buildings were on the outskirts of Carpenter, Alabama, and that put the issue square in the sheriff's department's jurisdiction.

Though Suzy wouldn't normally be the one to answer the call, and neither would Matt, they'd been only a street over when it had come in. She might be the chief deputy now, but her sense of obligation to her county hadn't changed with her promotion. Her soul was forever that of the young deputy she'd been the first day on the job. She took pride in every aspect of her work, even when it was something small.

"Thank goodness for cordless phones, sweet tea and an abundance of free time," Suzy said. "If she hadn't been snooping on the neighborhood from her porch, we might not have ever found him." She did another cursory look around the old saw manufacturing warehouse. The power had been off for years. Shadows dodged rays of light that filtered in from the hole past the rafters, and the few windows not broken or boarded up were coated in dust, pollen and mildew. Like the rest of the large, open room they were in. Suzy's sinuses pricked something awful. She'd have to take an allergy pill when they got back to her Tahoe. "I don't think this place gets visitors on a regular basis."

"That may be true, but I don't think he was dumped here *after* he was killed," Matt said, rising. He pointed to the trail of blood that had first grabbed her attention when they started searching the building. "For whatever reason, he was here, and so was his killer."

Suzy eyed the two doors at the end of the main room. The offices, most likely. They'd already passed the break room and bathroom up front.

"Let's finish going through the rest of this place before we dig any deeper into him," she said, pulling her gun back up. "If that *is* Gardner, then if all hell hasn't already broken loose, it will soon. We need to get out in front of this as fast as we can."

Matt agreed, and together they cleared the last two rooms before coming up to the back door. The lot the warehouse was on stretched wide but was empty. No people, no cars, just dirt, sun and a woman named June two blocks over, probably already gabbing to the whole town about what she'd heard. Which meant that whoever had killed the man inside had already left and had probably taken his car, too.

"I don't like this," Matt said at her side. "There's only two kinds of people who would kill Gardner."

"The brave and the idiots," she supplied.

He nodded.

"Either choice doesn't bode well for us. If you can kill the infamous Alabama Boogeyman, taking out a cop or two trying to solve his murder is easy pickings."

Suzy sighed. The beginnings of a headache started to throb, pressure wrapping around her right eye. It was going to be a long afternoon and night, she knew. Which meant that allergy pill needed to come sooner rather than later.

"I'm going to go pop some sinus meds and call Billy directly," she said after a moment of deliberation. "Go ahead and take some pictures of the body with your phone. While everyone knows I'm a fan of our *wonderful* Crime Scene Unit, we all know they can have lead in their feet. I'd rather have something we can refer to while we wait on them to process everything."

"You got it, boss."

Matt went back into the warehouse while Suzy went around it. Her head might have been focused and calm, but her gut muttered a warning. One she didn't listen to as she moved along the small strip of dead grass between the building and the side parking lot. Something felt off, but she wasn't sure what that something was.

Until she saw him.

A man wearing a jacket, despite the heat, hurried around the corner of the warehouse.

Between breaths, Suzy barely had time to register two things. She didn't recognize him.

And he had a gun.

Suzy reacted on instinct, pulling her service weapon up and yelling all at once.

"Drop it right now!"

The man was just as fast. His gun rose up in tandem, like they had planned the routine. It was the only reason Suzy didn't shoot right away.

She wasn't sure who had the upper hand.

"Whoa there, buddy," she said, hurrying over. "Sheriff's Department."

The man—thirties, dark hair, and thin-framed glasses—hesitated. Again, just like her, he didn't put down his gun. However, unlike her, he wasn't able to justify why he had one aimed at her in the first place. She was law enforcement. Who was he?

"Put your gun down!" Suzy yelled, voice a mix between grit and calm. She didn't want to agitate the man if she could help it. She'd prefer to talk him down if possible. The fact that she wasn't wearing a bulletproof vest was also a fact she was all too aware of. If she'd had the time, she would have cursed herself for leaving Matt before backup arrived.

But she didn't have the time. All thoughts were focused on the detective only a building away from her.

The man pulled his trigger before Suzy's brain could send the instruction to her finger to do the same.

The *bang* filled the afternoon air like it was a Fourth of July firecracker.

Suzy felt the weight of the world slam into her chest.

Then she was staring up at the sky.

Blue and white, and a little gray.

It was going to storm later. She hoped Justin didn't miss the bus. His mimi wouldn't be able to pick him up. Their car was still in the shop.

Another firecracker went off. Suzy tried to move to find the sound, but her body wasn't listening.

"Officer down!"

A face swam into view. It didn't belong to

Matt. It didn't belong to the man who'd shot her, either.

"You're going to be fine," he said. His voice was so smooth Suzy closed her eyes to savor it. "Hey, you stay with me, okay?"

But even though Suzy wanted to, she couldn't follow the command.

Her last thoughts before diving into the unknown were about her son, the rain and the stranger with a voice like warm velvet.

Chapter One

James Callahan thrust his hands deep into his pockets and braced against the cold. It was ninety-two degrees outside but only thirty-eight in the freezer. When he'd set up a time to meet a man named Sully the Butcher, James hadn't thought the place would be in a meat locker at the back of a restaurant downtown. It was a little too clichéd for his tastes. But he was nothing if not flexible.

"You wait here, old man. Or should I say, Padre. I'll go get 'em."

The young man—and that was being generous—was standing so close that the heavy scent of cheap aftershave invaded James's senses. Not in a good way. Whoever this kid was, James bet his dad would be coming home that night to a nearly empty bottle of the stuff. Assuming he had a dad who was around. Usually people who nicknamed themselves Queso and worked for a man called Butcher didn't have a normal home situation.

"I can see now why you have to make a reservation for this place," James quipped. He tilted his head to the hunk of meat hanging off a hook right behind them. "It's pretty crowded in here."

James busted out a wide grin at his own joke, but Queso wasn't amused. His exit was accompanied by an eye roll. The man guarding the door—with no nicknames that James knew of—kept his post without moving a muscle. Not that he needed to. Those muscles were thick and tattooed until there was more ink than bare skin. He didn't need a nickname. His purpose was to intimidate without saying a word.

James bet he was great at that. Sully might not be world famous, but he did a good job of keeping his name in the minds of the criminal underworld throughout the state. His network wasn't as big as that of the locals running the city of Kipsy a half hour away, but he didn't let that stop him from dipping his toes into the rest of the county's affairs. Still, regardless of Sully's lack of infamy, if anybody found themselves in his freezer with muscle guarding the door, they had every right to worry.

But while James wasn't a criminal, he wasn't exactly a nobody, either.

"Well, well, if it isn't the golden savior himself." On cue, a small-statured man walked in and spread his arms wide. James was surprised for several reasons. One, the man was wearing a pink-collared shirt, khaki shorts and golf shoes. Two, he looked closer to James's age of thirty-two than the old, weathered man he had been expecting. "Can't say I ever thought we'd meet like this, but who am I to question fate?"

He extended his hand, and James shook it.

"I have to admit, I thought you'd make me wait a lot longer in here," he said by way of greeting. "Make me sweat it, so to speak."

Sully laughed the thought off.

"I'm not trying to get information out of you, Mr. Callahan. In fact, I hear it's the other way around. And *that* is what interests me. As for the freezer?" He shrugged. "You know how the gossip wheel turns in this place? That doesn't stop just because we're not your average residents. If I don't keep up appearances, then that might send the wrong message to some of my associates. They might start questioning me. And I don't like questions."

"But you agreed to meet me."

Sully nodded. His hair, golden, thick and curly, was just another piece that didn't seem to fit the man or his reputation. Then again, James knew that images didn't always go hand in hand with reality.

"I don't like questions, but I do like mysteries," Sully informed him. "And it seems you walked into a big one."

"Gardner Todd's death."

Sully nodded, and his humor dropped a few pegs.

"What happened to him is…troubling," Sully admitted.

"That's a nice way to put it." James pulled a picture out of his pocket. "As is the man who presumably shot him."

Sully took the picture and was polite enough to examine it like he'd never seen the image of the dead man before. James bet there wasn't a cop or criminal who hadn't already seen it. It wasn't every day someone got the jump on the Alabama Boogeyman.

"You don't think he was the one who shot Gardner?" That surprised the man. "I thought the sheriff's department linked a gun he owned to the one that took out Todd."

"They did, and I do think he shot him," James conceded. "But what I don't get is why." He tapped the picture with his index finger twice. "This man's name is Lester Mc-Gibbon—"

"An unfortunate name," Sully interrupted to add.

"He lived in Atlanta and was suspected of corporate espionage but later cleared," he continued. "The man drove a Prius, had a soft spot for rescue dogs and took his son on fishing trips almost every weekend during the summer. He was white-collar crime through and through. So why did he come all the way to southern Alabama to kill the infamous Gardner Todd?"

James could feel his adrenaline spiking with every new thought. Even if he'd asked himself these same questions during many sleepless nights.

"So *that's* why you went looking for me," Sully said, a grin pulling up his lips. If they had been anywhere other than inside a freezer, James would have mistaken the man for some rich tourist, getting ready for a trip down to the beach a few hours away, perpetually retired and two seconds away from pulling out a margarita and donning a visor. "Because ole Lester was white-collar crime."

"It seems while everyone around here is still getting their hands dirty with armed robberies and drug deals, you've upgraded."

Sully's grin widened. Surprise mingled with pride lit his features, and his stomach rumbled with a laugh.

"Seems like the Bates Hill Savior is more well connected than I thought," he said. "And here I thought you only spent that fortune of yours on good deeds and photo shoots, not collecting rumors."

"They're not rumors if they're true," James pointed out.

Sully conceded to that with a shrug.

"I suppose not." The humor once again began to fizzle out. "Though I'd love to meet the people who provided my name and contact information to you. But I suppose you'll keep that to yourself."

James nodded. "You suppose correctly."

For a moment, James thought Sully would make it a point to find out the sources James had used to track the criminal. Sully might have taken his people off the streets and put them into offices, but that didn't undercut his abilities. Especially when he was trying to get something he wanted. You didn't get the nickname Butcher for no reason. However, he returned the picture to James and went back to the original topic.

"After the media released Lester's name, everyone in my line of work researched him. Not to mention, after he shot that woman cop, the entire county full of law enforcement tore through who he used to be. What makes you think I can answer questions all of those people couldn't? And why, for that matter, do you even care about what happened to Gardner Todd?"

James lowered his voice. Not to speak more quietly, but to convey what he said next was fact.

"Because I'd owe you one, and having a favor from James Callahan is gold in your particular line of work. The rest is none of your business."

A pregnant silence followed. It was just for show. James knew the moment the word "favor" had left his mouth that Sully was hooked. He was, at heart, a businessman first and foremost. He traded in deals and favors.

"That's quite the offer," he said after a moment. "No strings attached?"

James held up two fingers. "More like conditions," he said. "No one gets hurt or killed for this information."

Sully snorted. "You apparently haven't heard of my persuasive charm. Who needs brutality when you can just smile and get what you want?"

James fought the urge to roll his eyes and

continued. "And you call this number when you get anything." He pulled a piece of paper from his pocket and handed it over. "That's a private number. Only I should answer it. Which means you and/or any of your associates shouldn't feel the need to stop by the house. Sound good?"

He could tell Sully wasn't a man who was used to adhering to conditions he didn't set, but again, he was staring at the golden goose.

"Whatever you say, Mr. Callahan." The conversation was finished. They both knew neither one had any more to say. It was just theater when Sully motioned to the door. "I'll see what I can find."

Together they walked through the kitchen— past the staff and workers who didn't bat an eye—and to the back door that led into the employee parking lot. Queso stood next to the door, wearing slacks and a buttoned-up shirt that hung awkwardly off his thin frame. He zipped to attention as Sully neared, and James was reminded of being in boot camp back in the day. Respect and a little fear. The driving need to prove oneself.

James knew that need well.

"Take Mr. Callahan back to his car," Sully greeted him, then narrowed his eyes at the young man. "And make sure you go the speed limit this time. We're in small-town Alabama. Not street racing through the city trying to win a big score. The cops here won't have a hard time getting to you if you're blowing through the streets."

A look of quick shame followed by embarrassment crossed Queso's face. Sully cracked a grin. "Then again, I'm sure James here could sweet-talk his way out of it. Last I heard, he was on particularly good terms with law enforcement in these parts. Especially the sheriff's department."

This time James didn't fight the urge. He rolled his eyes.

"I'd stick to the speed limit if I were you."

Because even though he'd killed Lester Mc-Gibbon before he'd had the chance to send another bullet into Riker County's chief deputy, James had spent the last four months learning the hard truth about Suzanne Simmons.

She didn't like him.

Not one bit.

"No, sir." Suzy looked the sheriff dead in the eye and shook her head again. "There's no way I'm doing it."

Billy Reed chuckled. Just like he often did when he thought Suzy was being unreasonable. He'd made the same sound when he'd suggested she liked Jonathan Flynn in the seventh grade and even had the same look when he'd tried to set her up with Rick Carmichael right out of college. There were many more examples throughout their nearly lifelong friendship, but those two came to mind. Or rather, how she'd felt about those two specifically. It was a feeling she associated with the name

Billy was trying to attach her to now. She may have loved the sheriff like a brother, but that didn't mean she didn't think he'd lost his mind from time to time.

"I'm not asking you to date him," Billy pointed out, most likely knowing where her thoughts had gone. "I'm asking you to represent the Riker County Sheriff's Department at the town-hall social tonight."

"The social being held at the James Callahan estate," she interjected.

Billy chanced a look of mild exasperation.

"You know, he's not a bad guy. He single-handedly brought that town out of poverty. Not to mention he decided to make it his home. With all that money he could have his own island somewhere, but he chose Bates Hill, Alabama. That's got to count for something." Billy's brow drew in. The look didn't last long. "Though what he did for you is enough to say he's okay in my book for life. I don't understand why you're still so against him."

Suzy crossed her arms over her chest. She felt defiant. Protective. And she was trying to hide the scar between her breasts, even though her shirt was already covering it.

"I don't trust him for the same reasons you like him," she said simply. "His life trajectory doesn't make sense. A trust-fund kid, party animal, gives the tabloids enough material for years before disappearing. Then *bam!* He shows up to a smaller-than-small town to put it back on the map ten years ago with no reason other than he just wanted to do something good?" She shook her head. "Sounds like a movie I wouldn't even rent."

"Just because we don't know his life story doesn't mean you should write him off." Billy's face softened. "And just because Bates Hill and its residents are under our jurisdiction doesn't mean we need to know all of their secrets."

"True," she conceded. "But then, why was he out there that day, Billy? Why was James Callahan, of all people, at an abandoned saw manufacturing warehouse that just so happened to house the body of a murdered Gardner Todd?"

Billy's eyebrows knit together. No matter what he said next, Suzy knew he wasn't buying what he was selling. At least, not all the way.

"He was looking at real estate for one of his businesses. We even verified it with his attorney who showed up afterward. You already know that, and still you don't believe him."

It wasn't a question. Still, she responded to it.

"I believe that money can buy a lot of things," she said. "Including the loyalty of everyone around here. For all we know, his attorney spun the exact tale he wanted him to."

"So you think, what? James hired Lester McGibbon to kill Gardner and then shoot you?"

Suzy could tell that Billy didn't like being blunt about her being shot. It had been four months—four long months—and she still didn't like it, either. That bullet hadn't just hit her; it had very nearly killed her. Even now, she was still technically on leave from the department, unable to do field work for another month.

"No, I don't think he hired Lester," she admitted. "But I do think he's connected to Gardner. Somehow. And he's hiding it."

"Then what better reason than to go tonight? You can represent us *and* satisfy your curiosity."

Suzy tilted her head to see if she had heard him right. "You're saying you'd be okay with me asking him some questions?"

Billy nodded. "If you think there's something there, beyond the answers he's already given us all, then who am I to stop you?" He crossed his arms over his chest, his expression suddenly stern. "Just whatever prodding you do, please keep it *reasonable*."

Suzy couldn't help but smirk. "When have I ever been unreasonable?"

The sheriff was smart. He didn't answer.

QUESO WENT FIVE over the speed limit. James decided not to comment. Though the urge to get beneath the teen's skin almost won out.

Teen. That was what James really figured the dark-haired boy was. A teen who worked for an up-and-coming criminal organization that was tapping into white-collar crimes.

James wanted to give him a speech, to question his motives and push the boy to create different life goals, but then he remembered himself at that age and couldn't bring himself to deliver any lectures. What advice could he really give the boy that would ring true? He doubted repeating the speech James had gotten from his father all those years ago would light the fire that had moved him.

It had only been chance that, after his father had stopped yelling, the younger James had run into the bar where Corbin Griffin had been spending his last free night before taking off to San Antonio for basic training. The then twenty-year-old had shown James a way to prove himself outside of fame and fortune.

His joining the Air Force had surprised everyone; finding purpose and peace during his time with them had surprised him. Nine years after leaving, James still felt that swell of pride and gratitude for the time spent at his Special Operations job. Even when things had gotten hairy.

No, Queso needed his own Corbin Griffin. James doubted he would listen to him. Still, he wasn't going to say nothing. After the car rolled to a stop in the parking lot James's truck was in, he drew back and met the teen's stare.

"I don't know if Sully will get your help on what I'm looking for or not, but either way, it could be dangerous," he warned. "I suggest you stay away from it, but I'm sure that might only make you want to do it even more. Either way, if things get too hairy, you can reach me here." James pulled a card from his wallet. It had a different number on it than the one he'd given to Sully. "Or if you just want a different option altogether." He shrugged. "A few of my companies have scholarship programs that could use hardworking entrepreneurs. If that falls into your wheelhouse."

Queso cut a grin. "Haven't been called an entrepreneur before," he said. "Doubt a fancy title like that would even stick to someone like me. Don't you think?" Sarcasm. It blanketed his tone and posture. An invisible defense mechanism that James himself had used many times before in his youth. "Why don't you run along there, Padre, and leave your troubles to the boss?"

James got out of the car, hands up in defense. He left the card on the seat. Queso eyed it but didn't say anything. Maybe that was a good sign.

James finally got what he was hoping for. As he watched the little Miata take off down the road, thoughts of Suzanne Simmons were replaced by Gardner Todd.

And his killer.

If he could find out who wanted him dead, then maybe he could figure out Gardner's secret.

What did you want to tell me, brother?

Chapter Two

Suzy stood on the fringe of the crowd, pondering life.

Not in general, of course—she didn't have the patience for that one, or the right amount of caffeine in her, either—but on her own life. More important, the path that had led her, along with the Riker County Sheriff's Department, through the thickest of thicks and the thinnest of thins, all the way to standing on a rug that probably cost more than her two-bedroom rental.

It was a solid piece of decoration, almost as big as the foyer, and most likely heavy as the dickens. Without even attempting to lift the

thing, Suzy could feel its weight in her muscles. While she struggled with biting the bullet and buying a rug from Target, James Callahan had probably imported the thing from Sweden or somewhere equally expensive.

It made her want to grind her teeth. And make sure to keep her heels off it, if possible. Her mother had taught her to respect others' property. Even if she didn't respect the people who owned it.

Suzy sighed. She probably did need to cut the man who had saved her some slack. Whether he lived in a mansion or a shack shouldn't matter. He'd killed the man who had tried to kill her and then kept her from bleeding out in the dirt. He had also visited her in the hospital more than a few times. And when he couldn't come, he'd sent flowers. But no matter how nice the man was, it was hard to reciprocate when you knew he was lying.

"If you keep making that face, it might get stuck like that."

Suzy turned to a woman she'd been hoping to see when tasked with attending the social.

"Well, if it isn't Mrs. Reed, fashionably late, of course."

Billy's wife, Mara, beamed but didn't deny the accusation. Instead, she pointed to her protruding belly.

"I blame this kid of mine," she replied. "He's been tap-dancing on my bladder all day. You're lucky Leigh got us here when she did. We had to stop as soon as we got into town for a bathroom break."

Leigh Cullen was Mara's business partner and friend; together they ran an interior-design firm in Carpenter. Over the last year it had really taken off. They were currently designing an office-complex opening in the heart of Bates Hill. While Suzy knew Mara wasn't a fan of fancy parties and schmoozing, she knew it was hard to pass up a chance to meet James Callahan in his own home. He might have been a millionaire, but he rarely opened his house to the public.

Now Suzy couldn't help but wonder why.

A hush fell over the crowd before she could voice the question. The man of the hour appeared at the bottom of the stairs. Mistrust aside, Suzy felt her focus snap to attention.

James Callahan was a man you immediately thought about taking to bed. At least, Suzy did. He was tall, broad shouldered and admittedly good-looking. He wore his black hair short, cropped above the ears with some height at the top. It made him look authoritative and crisp. The consummate businessman. Yet the most attractive thing about him, for Suzy at least, was the charm behind every smile. *That* was his weapon. And that was what he wielded against the audience.

"First of all, I want to thank each and every one of you for coming out," he began, crystal-blue eyes scanning the people closest to him. Town council members, the local police and fire chiefs, and the mayor. The "it" people of Bates Hill. "I know it's been a stressful year, so I'm glad that I was able to offer up some levity by way of a party. You all work very hard to make sure this town stays afloat, and for that, I say thank you. And, as a token of my appreciation, instead of boring you with a speech, how about this—" He scooped a champagne flute off a waitress's tray at the base of the stairs and held it up. "Please make sure you take advantage of the food, drinks and live music on the patio! And have fun!"

He cast that charming smile out to the crowd as a whole. Its effect spread quickly. Soon even Mara was grinning.

"I think that man could read the alphabet and people would cheer," she whispered. Suzy snorted but didn't look away. James's gaze swept over her and then stopped. Heat rose from her belly, but she tried her best to keep it from reaching her cheeks.

"Why don't we go check out that food?" Suzy suggested, breaking the stare.

She might have had questions for the man, but now that she was here, she needed time to collect her thoughts.

It didn't help that James Callahan looked damn good in a suit.

THE PARTY WAS going better than he'd expected. It was nearing ten at night, and most of the attendees were still there, the party in full swing. They rotated in and out of the house, splitting their time between dancing, drinking and mingling. Most did, at least. James noticed the chief deputy kept the same glass and company for most of the party. Only briefly did she step out to talk to the police and fire chiefs before they left.

James was surprised at how much of his attention Suzanne kept without even trying. Even when carrying on his own conversations, he felt hyperaware of her presence. Like she was a glowing blip on his radar. A sound he always heard. A woman he couldn't ignore.

It was surprising at best, distracting at worst.

The way her brow furrowed when she was having a particularly serious talk and the small smile she wore when he bet she was trying to be polite were details that filtered in seconds after he found her again in the crowd. She seemed most comfortable with the sheriff's wife and her friend. When talking to them, her body language changed to become more relaxed, more animated. She'd tuck her long dark hair behind her ear or widen her brown eyes before laughing. He knew those eyes were the color of honey in the right light.

He'd looked down into them when holding her bleeding body.

James had wanted to approach her the moment he saw her in the crowd, but given the cold shoulder she'd shown him for the last four months, he decided to keep his distance. She didn't trust him, that much he could tell.

And she had every right.

Because Gardner Todd wasn't just some thug gunned down as justice for his past deeds.

He was James's brother.

"Mr. Callahan."

James turned to one of his friends who ran security for his events. Douglas was several inches shorter and as bald as a worn tire. James had once seen him body slam a man much bigger than either of them like it was a breeze.

"I told you not to call me that," James said after excusing himself from the group he had been in. "Makes me feel old."

Douglas snorted. "Just wait until I tell you who just called me and what it was about."

James already felt the sigh coming out of his mouth before Douglas could explain.

"Let me guess—it starts with Chelsea and ends with pain-in-my-backside."

Douglas laughed. "You got it, boss."

James rolled his eyes but didn't feel any real

annoyance. He flipped his smartwatch around to see the date.

"Considering her bio lab test was last week, I'm assuming this call has something to do with the grade she got on it?"

But Douglas kept tight-lipped. "She wants you to call her back after the party," he said. "And told me I'm not allowed to tell you one way or the other."

James couldn't help but laugh. "I should worry how easily my sister wraps you around her finger, but then again, I'm there, too." He clapped Douglas on the shoulder. "I'll go call her now. I didn't help her study for that lab every weekend for the last month for nothing. Keep this party going in my absence. If anyone asks where I went, just tell them I'm in the wine cellar getting toasted."

It was Douglas's turn to laugh as James left the main room and went to the small set of stairs in the kitchen. He bounded up them two at a time and headed toward his office. He pulled out his cell phone and was calling before he even reached the doorway.

SUZY WATCHED AS James was pulled from his conversation by a member of the security team. Whatever the situation was, it didn't appear to be serious, yet after they were done the man of the hour left the party. Curiosity filled her so quickly that before she had time to process what she was doing, Suzy had excused herself from Mara's side and followed the millionaire.

Billy's request that she question James within reason repeated in the back of her mind as she waited a few seconds before going up the stairs behind him. She walked slowly to keep her heels from making a sound until she was standing in the upstairs hallway. If James caught her now, she figured she could come up with a valid excuse for following him. Yet she found her feet stalling on the landing.

What exactly was she hoping to find?

Did she really expect the man to buckle beneath her questions, giving up answers that she had been looking for?

Suzy felt a swirl of adrenaline in her gut. Something she'd often experienced out in the field. A feeling she'd been missing for the last four months. For one small moment, she reveled in how it made her heart beat faster, her senses more alert and her mind more clear.

If James really *was* involved with what had happened to Gardner Todd, then that meant he was someone to exercise caution around. Add in his fortune and connections and being on his own home turf?

She was putting herself in a dangerous situation.

She was being careless.

Like not wearing her vest four months ago.

Suzy turned toward the window and stopped before going back down the stairs. The scar between her breasts heated up. She fisted her hands, remembering the look on her son's face when she'd woken up in the hospital. He'd just turned ten and was trying his hardest to prove to her that he was old enough to keep it together. He'd been trying to be strong. For her. For himself. It wasn't until she promised him it was okay to cry that he'd broken down on her lap.

The adrenaline spiked in her belly. Her nails bit into the palms of her hands.

Suzy never wanted to put him in that situation again. Not if she could help it. Not when she could avoid it.

She'd figure out what James was hiding, but not like this. Not creeping around in the shadows of his house. Not by putting herself in compromising positions.

No, she'd figure it out another way.

A *safer* way.

Suzy nodded to herself and fully intended on going back downstairs to the party, but movement outside the window caught her eye. The side lawn wasn't lit up like the back patio, but there was enough glow from the hanging lights that she could just make out someone moving toward the house. Slowly and not at all steadily.

Limping.

She sucked in a breath as the man moved closer. The light from the kitchen window caught him.

That was when she saw the blood.

He was covered in it.

The swirl of adrenaline in her stomach upgraded to a storm.

Chapter Three

Suzy hurried down the stairs, not minding this time that her high heels hit each step and sounded off like thunder crashing in the night sky. The chatter from the party in the center of the house kept going, uninterrupted. That meant no partygoer or security guard had spotted the bleeding man.

The cop in her rattled off four instantaneous questions in her head as she stepped toward the side door.

Who was the man?

What had happened to him?

Why had it happened to him?

Why was he at James Callahan's town social?

No answers came as she flew out into the night and straight toward the unknown. The lights from the backyard cast a glow across the small patio and garden, but were still too weak to show her any new clues to help answer any questions. The blood was there, dark against his face and arms, but she couldn't be sure *where* it had come from. His struggle to walk made her assume it was at least partly his.

"Whoa there, buddy," she said, trying for soothing tones while staying cautious. She went at him with one arm out, like a deputy trying to direct traffic, while the other hung back so her hand was never too far from the holster hidden against her thigh. If she needed to get to her gun fast, she could. However, it would be interesting for any bystanders, considering she'd probably have to rip the dress to get to it. A small price to pay for being prepared, but still, she hoped she wouldn't have to ruin it. Not only because she thought it was beautiful, but also because it was on loan from Mara.

The man's head moved enough that, even in the poor light, Suzy knew he was looking at her. Now she was close enough to guess that he wasn't a party guest *or* security. Instead of a suit, he wore jeans and a graphic T with some band's logo on it in neon orange. In fact, the more she tried to find the source of his bleeding, the more Suzy wondered if he was a man at all. He seemed too young.

"Inside," he groaned out, voice surprisingly strong. "I need to get inside."

He lurched forward. Suzy's reaction time since the accident had slowed, but she still managed to dance away from touching the blood on his arm. She latched on to his wrist instead.

"What's going on?" she tried. "I'm with the sheriff's department. I can help."

The man reacted like she'd stung him. Suzy felt his arm muscles coil a split second before he pulled out of her grip. The sudden momentum, plus the fact that she was unaccustomed to wearing heels, threw her off balance enough that she was forced to let go or fall.

"Get away from me," he hissed. "Where's Mr. Callahan?"

He turned back to the house, eyes wild, but that didn't mean she was done with him. Suzy took one step closer, pivoted enough to bring her back leg forward and kicked out at the man. The sound of fabric splitting was followed by a grunt as her foot connected with his stomach. She wasn't trying to hurt him, but she *was* trying to control him.

He toppled over and hit the ground. Suzy didn't wait for him to get his bearings. She flipped off her shoe and pressed her foot against his shoulder to keep him down.

"I'm Chief Deputy Simmons," she announced. "You *will* tell me what's going on and you will do so in a calm manner."

The man's eyes widened and flicked toward the house before coming back to her.

"I need to talk to Mr. Callahan," he said. "Right now!"

He bucked up against her foot, but Suzy wasn't having it. She applied enough pressure to keep him down.

"What you need is medical attention," she pointed out. "You're covered in blood."

The man twisted beneath her weight. "No, I don't," he managed around his squirming. "What I need—is to—talk to—Mr. Callahan."

Suzy's curiosity overrode her caution. She leaned over, careful not to press against him too hard, and fixed the man with a stare he couldn't misinterpret as something he could ignore. Even in the darkness.

"Tell me why, or I'm calling in the cavalry right now."

This time he didn't fight back. That didn't mean he was calm, though—not by any means.

"They found him," he practically yelled. "And now they're going after him!"

Suzy tilted her head on reflex, but she never got to ask another question. Someone else beat her to it.

"Going after who? Me?"

Suzy's hand was at her holster in a flash. The cool night air moved across her upper thigh, confirming that she had, indeed, already ripped the dress. She didn't let up off the man as she turned to the new voice. Though it wasn't new to her at all.

"Going after who?" James repeated. His expression was hard, but Suzy couldn't read what emotion made it so.

The man struggled against her foot again, but this time Suzy let him up. She kept her hand on the butt of her gun.

"I don't know," he started, with eyes only for James. "But—but Sully gave me this address to get to you." He fumbled a hand into his pocket. If he hadn't been wearing tight jeans, showing he wasn't carrying a gun, Suzy would have pounced. But now that James was here, her captive's earlier feistiness had seemingly vanished. When he pulled out a paper and handed it to James, his hand shook. "He said it's what you're looking for. New information. I don't know who they are or who they're going after. He didn't have time to tell me."

Suzy didn't have to know the situation to understand that the stakes had just risen. James looked over the paper. His eyebrows threaded together.

Maybe he didn't know the situation, either. Confusion blanketed his expression.

"What happened to you?" he asked. This time, she heard the concern before she saw it. It was familiar in nature. James knew the man. "And who did it?"

Suzy half expected the man to remain silent, as he had with her, but again, having James there seemed the key to unlocking answers. The man took a deep breath.

"You were right," he said. "It was too dangerous." He raised one hand up toward the little light they had. Blood. Some was dry. Some wasn't. "It isn't mine," he said. "The blood isn't mine."

Suzy glanced at James. He still looked as confused as she felt.

"Whose blood is it?" she had to ask.

The man's gaze stuck to his hand.

James crouched down so he was at eye level with the other man. "Queso, whose blood is it?" Suzy didn't have a chance to question the name. She was holding her breath for an answer. "Queso?"

James reached out and grabbed his shoulder. It did the trick in focusing him.

"It's Sully's," Queso finally answered, voice low. "I don't even know if he's still alive. He made me run when the shooting started. He told me that getting you that address was too important." He let out an exhalation. It deflated him. "Padre, he said you're already running out of time."

"Okay, I've heard enough."

Suzy placed her hands up in defeat. She wasn't about to let this show go on any more. The story was lost on her, everyone's motivations just as hazy. She'd made a promise to herself not to willingly walk into situations exactly like the one she'd just walked into. Having a powwow with a man who had just confessed the blood he was covered in was not his own? A man who had limped from the dark of night to James Callahan's estate instead of to the police?

It was too much.

"I'm calling this in."

"You can't," Queso said hurriedly. His haze had been replaced with sheer panic in seconds. It hit every syllable in his words. "If anyone knows I talked to the cops, I'm done for." He shook his head and turned to James.

"And you'll be out of even more time. Please, Padre, don't let her call them in."

Suzy grabbed her discarded high heel and tried to cool her mounting anger before it came to a head.

"I *am* the law," she reminded him. "And no amount of money is going to erase that fact. Now, can you walk to the house or do we need to carry you?"

Queso flapped his mouth open and closed. James answered for him.

But not with what she wanted to hear.

"Maybe we should go inside and take a moment to think this through, Suzanne."

If there was one thing Suzy disliked more than a man trying to tell her how to do her job—or when *not* to do it—it was a man calling her Suzanne.

"Either call me Suzy or Chief Deputy Simmons," she snapped. "And there's nothing to talk through. Something is going on, you're in the middle of it and I'm going to get answers this time around. Honest ones."

She grabbed Queso's wrist and pulled up. James helped but kept talking.

"I need to go see what's at this address. *Now*, not later," he tried. "You heard him. I'm running out of time."

Suzy whirled around as the side door banged open. The man James had been talking to before he'd gone upstairs had a towel in his hand.

"Listen, *Suzy*, this is my head of security, Douglas. Let him watch Queso until we know what's here." He shook the paper with the address on it. "Then we can do whatever you feel we need to do. Please."

All three men looked up at her.

"You're out of your mind," she exclaimed. "A bloody guy limps to your party and gives you an address, and then you want to go off without anything else to go on? Even if I wasn't law enforcement, I would think that's crazy."

Then James did something that surprised

her. He almost closed the space between them, his blue, blue eyes never leaving hers.

"I know you don't trust me," he said, voice low. "You don't believe that I just happened to be out there that day...and you're right."

Suzy felt her eyes widen.

"Then why were you?" she had to ask.

Would it be this simple to get her answer?

James angled his body slightly, as if he didn't want Douglas to hear what he had to say next. Suzy couldn't help herself. She leaned in a fraction.

"Because Gardner Todd, my brother, asked me to meet him there." Before Suzy could react, he continued. "He said he needed to tell me something important. I never learned what that was, never even had a clue, either. Until this." Suzy glanced at the paper in his hand. "Listen, I'm not like my brother, but I am like you. I want answers, too. So let's go get some before it really *is* too late."

There was so much to process that Suzy

couldn't land on any one point or question. In part, that was because of the pure urgency behind his plea. It bled through his words and into her. So sincere. So *real*.

James wasn't the only one surprised when she nodded.

"Okay, I'll go with you," she agreed. "But I'm going to need answers on the way. And, Mr. Callahan, if you lie to me again, no one will be able to help you. Not your money, not your lawyer, not even the entire town of Bates Hill. Got it?"

He nodded. "Yes, ma'am."

Chapter Four

Suzy shook her head. She might have followed the millionaire to and into his truck, but she was still having a hard time believing what he'd said.

"Gardner Todd had no family," she said. "At least, nothing in his files ever said that at any point he had a brother. Let alone that you're him."

The truck hit a series of bumps that rocketed Suzy off the seat. James threw his hand out to steady her. His palm pressed against her rib cage. Through the thin material of the dress, she could feel the heat of his skin. It momentarily distracted her.

"Like you guessed, some people will do anything for the right price," he said, unaware that his contact had put a hiccup in her thoughts. "And my father was all about knowing what somebody's right price was. It was easy to keep Gardner out of the spotlight. Easier, too, when Gardner ran away at sixteen."

"But why?" Suzy interjected. James pulled his hand back, setting it on the steering wheel. The dark night kept flying by the windows. "Why would he erase Gardner like that?"

A small smile pulled at the corner of James's lips. In the dark of the cab, Suzy couldn't tell if it was a happy one. Given the subject matter, she doubted it.

"Gardner wasn't a crazy kid, if that's what you're after. But he drove our dad crazy. And it went both ways. My dad wasn't the easiest man to get along with, and for whatever reason, Gardner got the short end of the stick with him. They never had one big fight, just a hundred little ones. It was like everything he did rubbed Dad the wrong way." He shrugged. "And there's only so much anger and disappointment and resentment you can shell out on a kid before they eventually either become the person you made them out to be or a completely different person, despite what you tried to make them."

"You're talking about Gardner Todd here," Suzy said, still in disbelief that he was related to the man next to her. "The Alabama Boogeyman. The fixer who gets hired by the highest bidder. Notorious across the state for his role as being basically the best criminal handyman."

James shrugged again. "I never said he was perfect."

The truck slowed enough to hook a right. Beneath the tires was nothing but dirt and rock. They were in backcountry and only getting farther into it.

"If he really was your brother, father issues

aside, why run away and give up a fortune? Especially if he could have inherited it."

The smile—and whatever it meant—disappeared from James's lips.

"I never got to ask. I was thirteen when he left. He sent birthday cards, but the last time I talked to him in person was a few days after Dad passed."

"But you were going to meet him at the warehouse."

James stiffened, then nodded.

"In the last few years he'd call me occasionally to talk. Nothing devious or anything. Just about how I was doing and checking up on our sister, Chelsea, mostly. Honestly, I think he regretted not having a relationship with her, but as you've pointed out, he was in with the worst kind of crowd. And he knew it. He never tried to come around while I raised her, and I never invited him to."

"Until four months ago," Suzy offered.

"He called and I knew something was off.

He said there was something he had to talk to me about. In person. Something important." James tightened his grip on the steering wheel. His knuckles turned white. A muscle in his jaw twitched. "By the time I got there…well, you know."

Suzy fidgeted in her seat. "So you have *no* idea what he wanted to tell you?"

He shook his head. "I have no idea what he wanted or why he chose to meet there. Or who wanted him dead. I might not be in law enforcement, but that doesn't mean I haven't heard about his reputation. If someone wanted him dead, it was a bold move. One not many would make. Especially not Lester McGibbon. At least, not on his own."

Suzy and Matt had already agreed on that point. Nothing in Lester's history suggested he would go from white-collar crime to taking on Gardner. Someone either bold or stupid had ordered the hit and gotten the man to do it.

"You think what Gardner wanted to talk

to you about was related to his death," she guessed.

James reduced the truck's speed and leaned forward to get a better look ahead.

"When the Alabama Boogeyman has a secret for you and then gets shot three times before he can tell?"

"It's hard not to connect the two," she admitted.

"Damn hard."

He motioned out the windshield, but Suzy was already pulling out her gun. The country road was funneling them toward a house in the distance. Not a farmhouse—it was too small, and there was nothing else around the property that suggested the owners dealt with animals or crops—but something more quaint. One lone exterior light hung over the front door. There were no cars around.

"You've never been to this house?" she asked, already knowing the answer. In profile, she could see the way his brows pinched together. Along with her, he was seeing the house for the first time.

"I've never been here," he confirmed. "I didn't even know there were houses this far out here."

Bates Hill might have been a small town, but its country land ran for a good chunk of miles. As far as Suzy could recall, she hadn't been out here, either. Which meant she needed to be on her A game.

As easy as it had been to not trust James during the last four months, she couldn't help but believe that *he* believed the tip he'd gotten was genuine.

Suzy took the safety off her weapon.

James didn't stop in front of the house. Instead, he drove a circle around it and parked facing the road they'd come from. No one stirred inside.

"Ready, Chief Deputy Simmons?" There was a hint of excitement in his voice. It matched the small dose of adrenaline building in her.

The danger of the unknown. The promise of getting justice. All in a day's work.

"Yes, but at the first sign of trouble I'm calling in the cavalry. Got it?"

James snickered. "I wouldn't have thought otherwise."

They got out of the truck and fell into a surprisingly comfortable rhythm. James led the way to the door and knocked, and when no one answered, he stepped to the side. He tried the doorknob. It turned, but he didn't open the door. Instead, he gave Suzy a look that made pride for her job swell in her chest. She pushed her shoulders back, brought her gun up, and looked ahead and nodded. James opened the door wide and waited as Suzy pushed in first, gun ready.

"Riker County Sheriff's Department!" she yelled, quick on her feet.

No one yelled or jumped out, but Suzy didn't slow. She went through the living area as soon as James turned on the light. No sign of anyone. She moved to the one bedroom and the attached bathroom, flipping on the rest of the lights as she went.

"It's clear," she called after checking the closets. She holstered her gun and went back to the living room. "Anything you recognize?"

The room was small and open to the kitchen. A modest furniture set centered the room while a bookshelf took up half the wall near the front door. James stood in front of it, scanning the books and odds and ends it housed.

"I don't know," he answered after moving to the next shelf. "Nothing so far. No pictures or anything that I think would constitute a secret worth killing to protect." He reached over and pulled out a book. "Unless someone really didn't like *Romeo and Juliet.*"

Suzy walked to a chest against the wall and opened it. It contained a few handwoven blankets and a shoe box. Carefully she lifted the small box out.

"Do you think this is where he lived?" she

had to ask, taking the lid off. "Gardner, I mean. Did he ever tell you where he stayed?" The box was filled with blank envelopes and a pen.

"That's just another question I never asked. Though I assumed he had a place north of Birmingham. Definitely not here."

"Maybe this place *is* the secret."

Suzy placed the box to the side and pulled the blankets out. She tossed them onto the couch.

"A secret about what?" James asked, his focus still on the bookcase. "That whoever stayed here liked isolation and Shakespeare?" Suzy could hear the frustration in his voice.

"Your source could have been pulling your leg," she pointed out.

He turned and their eyes met. Blue glass. Sharp and clear. "You saw Queso. Do *you* think he was lying?"

"I think he was scared and confused," she admitted. "He might have misinterpreted what he saw or was simply given the wrong information on purpose."

James didn't agree. He didn't even have to shake his head to get that point across. He squared his shoulders defensively. "My source wouldn't do that."

He didn't elaborate past that, and Suzy didn't push. He stalked past her into the bedroom.

James might have told her one of his secrets, but he certainly had more up his tailored sleeves. Maybe jumping into his truck without a second thought hadn't been her best move. Answers be damned.

They spent the next several minutes in silence, both working their rooms. Suzy checked the side tables, went back over the bookcase and started pulling out kitchen cabinets and drawers. Whoever lived in the house had either left in a hurry or hadn't been there in a while. Almost everything was cleaned out of the kitchen.

Almost being the operative word.

"James!"

"Suzy!"

Suzy jumped and turned as they spoke at the same time. James walked into the living room, holding a cloth in his hand.

"I would say 'jinx,' but I don't think it works like that," he said. The joke didn't hold any humor. James's expression was blank. "I found this in the dresser. It was hung up between the drawers."

He held the cloth up. Only it wasn't just a cloth.

It was a small onesie. One with a rubber ducky sewn in the middle.

Suzy's heart began to race. She stepped to the side to show what she'd found.

"It was at the back of the cabinet. I almost didn't see it."

James's eyes widened. He picked up the can. His expression gave nothing away. "'Formula,'" he read.

"*Baby* formula," she said, wanting to be crystal clear in what they were seeing.

"Baby formula," he repeated. She watched as he looked between the canister and the rubber-ducky onesie. They clearly didn't have answers, but she did have a few guesses.

"If this house isn't a secret, then maybe whoever was here is." She took the onesie from his hand. His gaze followed it. "And I'm assuming Gardner never mentioned a baby to you."

James shook his head. "No, he didn't."

"So, maybe he was hiding someone here? Someone with a baby? Or—"

"Or the baby is his," James interrupted. And his blank expression gained some emotion. Anger. Concern. Something else.

Something Suzy found she wanted to combat or soothe. She wasn't sure which. He *was* James Callahan, after all. A man she'd spent the last four months distrusting with a vengeance.

"I was going to say *or* this has nothing to do with Gardner, and whoever your source was wanted you here. Where there just so happened to be a baby at one point in time." She motioned to the rest of the drawers and cabinets, all open and mostly empty. "We still have no evidence that Gardner is even linked to this place. Other than, like you said, the owner seems to love isolation and Shakespeare. But I can't imagine he's the only person in the world to like both. That could be nothing more than a coincidence."

James opened his mouth, but whatever he was originally going to say died on his tongue. In a move that was so quick Suzy reached for her gun, James spun on his heel and hurried to the bookcase. He grabbed a book and opened it, determined. He shook his head.

"This may or may not have been his place, but Gardner definitely was here at one point." He held the book up, cover open. From her spot, Suzy could see handwriting against the first page. "He didn't like Shakespeare, but our mother did." He tapped the signature. "She always signed the inside of her books." He smiled. "I thought Dad gave them all away when she passed."

Suzy looked down at the onesie in her hand. The rubber ducky was wearing a blue ribbon around its neck.

A not-so-great feeling started to mix with the adrenaline in her stomach. Confusion was never fun, especially when it came with urgency.

"So, if Gardner stayed here with a baby—"

The window next to the front door exploded in a spray of glass. Suzy flung herself to the floor as another window burst out of its frame. She didn't have to be on her feet to know what was happening.

Whatever Gardner Todd's secret was, it looked like whoever was outside was also looking for it.

And they'd brought guns.

THE FIRST SHOT pushed him to the floor. The second had him wishing he'd brought his gun in from the truck. The third, fourth, fifth and—hell, he'd lost count—the rest of the bullets that were plugging into the house had James low and crawling to the kitchen, hoping he and the chief deputy weren't about to have a repeat of what happened at the warehouse.

Suzy was on the floor but, thankfully, not on her back this time. He gave her a once-over the best he could, given bullets were still flying. No blood or wounds that he could see. She lifted her head up enough to meet his eye as the cabinets above them splintered.

James didn't waste any more time. He closed the distance between them and covered her with his body. She didn't fight him. Which was good, because whoever was outside wasn't done.

Once again James lost count in the barrage of bullets that continued to come. There was definitely more than one gunman. In fact, he guessed they were being shot at from both sides of the house, the way it was crumpling around them.

If they managed to not get shot, the house falling apart just might do them in.

James moved his head so his lips were right next to Suzy's ear. "How much ammo do you have on you?"

"Not enough!" she yelled back. "Only the clip in my gun."

James said a few choice words born of frustration. He just hoped their enemy's show of force would empty their own reserves. Maybe they could get away with only one clip. It wasn't like they had much choice. From what he'd already seen of the house, it was empty of anything worth fighting with. If the house was Gardner's, and James realized he was already convinced it was, then at one point it had to have been well stocked with weapons. But now?

Now it was picked clean.

James was still trying to come up with a better plan than trying to take on what sounded like an army with only one clip when the gunfire finally stopped. The house continued to groan in the aftermath. Half of a cabinet door broke free and bounced off his back. There was no time to survey the damage.

"You okay?" James asked, voice low.

"I will be when we get out of here," she replied hurriedly. James liked the fire in her voice.

He moved into a half crouch, careful to keep out of the view of the windows. Suzy followed until they were at the back door. Whatever slugs their mystery gunners had been slinging had trashed it and the windows. The walls were mostly intact.

And probably the only reason they were still alive.

James moved to the other side of the door as Suzy took up a spot next to it. He had a moment of déjà vu. He held up his finger to keep her quiet and peered out of one of the bullet holes.

Less than a second later, he was certain that one clip was not enough.

He reached out and took Suzy's wrist.

"We need to hide," he said urgently. *"Now."*

Chapter Five

The world around them was moving so fast, but James couldn't help feeling as if they were moving as slow as dirt. It didn't help that not one or two but at least six men were closing in on the house from the backyard alone. It also didn't help that the only hiding place he could think of was hard as the dickens to get to. At least, when that hiding place was the attic and you were hopped up on adrenaline and trying to get a beautiful woman in a slinky dress up into that attic.

With no ladder.

As soon as he pulled the string down and the door opened, James had Suzy by the waist and was shimmying her upward. Under different circumstances, he might have taken a beat to appreciate the way her body felt beneath his hands. Just like Suzy might have, under different circumstances, had some words to say when his hands cupped her backside with vigor, pushing her up until she could pull herself the rest of the way. As it was, they both kept their mouths clamped shut.

The moment Suzy cleared the opening, she spun around and held out her hand. James was already one step ahead of her. He jumped, thanked his lucky stars that he was a tall man and managed to grab the lip of the opening. Before he could start pulling himself up, a sound he'd been hoping not to hear until he was hidden exploded through the house.

Someone had kicked the front door off its hinges.

James pulled all the way up, once again was thankful that one thing he'd kept from his Air Force days was his workout routine.

Suzy grabbed his back and then his belt. Then it was his backside she was cupping.

Another bang sounded as what was left of the back door was opened with force.

James grabbed on to the closest beam and pulled with all of his might. The moment his feet cleared the opening, Suzy reached through the space and grabbed for the string attached to the door. James twisted around and put his arms around her waist in time to keep her from falling out. After two swipes she got it, and together they closed it as quickly and quietly as they could.

With absolutely no time to spare.

No sooner was the door in place than a series of voices could be heard in the room beneath them. James and Suzy didn't dare move. He didn't even release his hold around her middle, and she didn't complain.

"Check the closet and bathroom," one man barked.

"If they're in here, we got them already,"

said another. His drawl was pure syrup. "Nobody can take that much lead."

"They can if you're crap with your aim," said another man. The voice was a higher pitch than the other two. Younger. "You should have let me do the shooting, and not Ryan and skunk for brains here."

"I was fifty-fifty on killing him or keeping him alive," the first man said. "Either outcome I can work with."

"No one's in here," the person with the Southern drawl called from the bathroom. "The house is empty."

"So, whose truck is that, and where are they?" It was the third man who asked, and something in the back of James's mind rattled around at his voice. It sounded familiar. If only he could *see* the three people beneath them.

"It could have been Sully's boy who got free earlier," the first said. "Came out here to warn Hank that we were coming and left on his bike. Might explain how they got away before we got here."

James couldn't help but tense up. He felt Suzy turn her head enough to look at him. A lot of good that did in the dark. While there might have been more than a few Hanks in Alabama, James knew of only one who would be tangled up with his brother. If Hank had been at the house, then there was no doubt Gardner had once been there, too.

"Well, what do we do now?" the drawler asked. "We got all the boys here and no one to question."

The sigh was so loud, James heard it as though the man was in the attic with them.

"Looks like we'll just have to hunt down Hank and make *him* tell us where he hid the boy before anyone else finds out Gardner Todd's son is out there missing."

If James tensed at the mention of Hank's name, he turned into a statue at this new information.

Gardner had a son?

He had a nephew?

Suddenly everything fell into place. The urgency to meet in person. The secret he'd been trying to tell James.

Gardner had a son.

A son who was in trouble now.

Rage, pure as pollen in the spring, filled James so quickly that he had half a mind to open the attic door and bring down a heap of pain on the men in the bedroom. Had they been the ones who had ordered Lester to kill his brother? Why were they after the boy? What were they planning on doing with him after they found him?

Every question pushed adrenaline into James's muscles.

In the darkness of the attic, all he saw was red.

And then that red cooled.

Suzy moved her hand onto the arm he had around her stomach. Her fingers delicately wrapped his forearm. Then, in the smallest of movements, she brushed her thumb across his skin.

The rage in him quieted, and sense returned to him.

Jumping out and taking on the unknown number of armed men would only get him killed, and her, too. And then his nephew would still be in danger.

James squeezed her side to let her know he'd gotten the message.

"Go get Zach and the boys, and tell them to go ahead and hit the road," the first man said. He must have been the one in charge at the moment. James committed his voice to memory. "Keep your phones on," he called as one of the men's footsteps went back into the living room.

"What do you want me to do?" the third man asked. Not the guy with the Southern accent. Again, James felt like he could almost place the man's voice. "I mean, do we even know where Hank is?"

"No, but Sully does."

"I thought he was gone. In the wind."

"Doesn't mean we can't get him back. The sorry SOB has a lot of problems, but his worst one is how he feels about his people. We find that boy he took a bullet for, and I bet we could smoke him out."

"If Sully hasn't already bought a one-way ticket to the great fire pit in the ground."

The first man laughed. It sounded like nails against a chalkboard.

"He may be soft, but Sully isn't about to let a bullet do him in."

Car doors shut in the distance. An engine turned over.

"And what if he doesn't know where Hank is? Heck, what if Hank is already on his way out of the state with the boy?"

Zach, the boys and the man with the Southern twang must have been leaving. James tried to split his attention, to see if he could hear if one or two vehicles were driving off, but he very much wanted the same answers as the unknown third man did.

"You may not have been in for long enough to know about Hank, but I used to run with him a few years back. He's not a stationary man, and definitely not a fan of the state. He came back for a reason. He won't leave until he's done whatever he needed to, and my guess is it wasn't being the father to Gardner Todd's kid. Now, let's start with his old woman in—"

Music—the chorus of the song "It's Raining Men," to be precise, courtesy of James's sister and how hilarious she thought it was to try to embarrass him when she called—filled the attic around them. He and Suzy both reached for his coat pocket and his phone, lit up and blaring.

"What the—"

James wrapped his hand around the phone and pulled Suzy up and farther into the darkness, just as a shot sounded up through the attic door.

"We need light!" she yelled. No point in trying to pretend no one was home when The Weather Girls were belting out one of their most famous hits.

James held up the phone, giving them some light. Another bullet embedded itself in the roof above them. As soon as Suzy could see, she was playing hopscotch across the ceiling beams. The last thing they needed was to fall into the bedroom.

"Whoever you are, you're screwed!" yelled one of the men. James didn't have the time to figure out which one it was. He canceled Chelsea's call and used the phone as a flashlight.

The attic ran the length of the house and was by no means spacious. They hunched and clung to roof beams as they hurried to get out from above where the men were.

Not that that would make much difference when they decided to walk into the living room and unload a few more rounds into the ceiling.

"How close is the truck to the house?" Suzy asked James. A ripping sound pulled his attention to her dress just in time to watch the tear that was already there split all the way up to her hip. Lord have mercy—if they weren't running for their lives, James would have had to really think on the lacy number she was wearing beneath it.

"How close is the—" he repeated.

Suzy cut him off. "The vent!"

James followed her line of sight to the attic vent at the end of the house. With a jolt of excitement, he understood.

"Close enough," he said.

Another two bullets shot up behind him, too close for comfort. Suzy must have sensed it. The moment she got to another beam, she turned toward him, brandishing her gun.

"Move!" she yelled.

James didn't have to be told twice. He hurried around her and kept going toward the vent while she did some shooting of her own. He counted four shots by the time he made it to the beam closest to the vent.

Two bullets answered from the men below. James turned, worried she'd been hit.

"Hurry!" she shouted at him.

Holding two roof beams to steady himself the best he could in the small space, James pulled back his leg and then kicked out at the attic vent with all he had. The planks of wood splintered beneath the force. Suzy sent another few rounds beneath them while he kicked out again. Before he could clear the last two planks, he could already see the truck beneath them.

"This is going to hurt," he called over his shoulder. He moved his phone to allow more light to help her get the rest of the way to him.

"Not as much as getting shot," she bit back. "Trust me."

He wasn't about to argue.

He broke the last board, until all that was left was a hole they'd have to squeeze through. But, like Suzy said, it was better than the alternative.

"As soon as you hit the truck bed, I'm gunning it. So make sure you buy us some time with those bullets," he said.

"Yes, sir." Suzy nodded, turned and unloaded her clip into the floor.

As soon as the last bullet left her barrel, James moved through the hole that used to be the attic vent, grabbed on to its sides, said a quick prayer and pushed off.

WHEN SUZY WAS FIFTEEN, she had dared Billy to jump off the Wendigo Bridge on their way home from school. It wasn't that high above the water, but tall enough that Billy wasn't having any of it. By the time she'd decided to stop ragging him about it, Tommy Wexler and his cute older brother had shown up. The way

Suzy had seen it then, she'd had no choice at that point. She *had* to jump.

She still remembered how her stomach had turned to nothing but butterflies as she stood on the old railing and looked down at the water. Billy had still been spouting concern, but promised he'd try to fetch her if she started drowning. The Wexler boys weren't as concerned, but said a few things that made her believe they'd be impressed if she did, indeed, go through with it. So she'd taken that first step without hesitation.

What Suzy never told Tommy Wexler—or Billy, for that matter—was that she'd seen her friend Melanie do the same thing the previous summer on a dare. It was a scary drop, but as long as she tucked her legs in and held her nose, she'd be fine. But Melanie had told Suzy that the real secret was in knowing you'd be fine before you ever did it. Confidence was key, she'd said.

Now, no longer a teen trying to impress a

boy, Suzy realized that the key had never been confidence. It had been youthful stupidity.

And, boy, did she feel stupid jumping off a house in an attempt to hit the back of a truck with a nine- or ten-foot drop in between the two.

She felt a slight fizzle of confidence spring up when James hit his target and none of his bones snapped in half. At least, none that she heard.

James landed in the truck bed on his feet, and a second later he was out and over the side. The moment he flung open the driver's-side door, Suzy held her breath and followed.

If she hadn't abandoned her high heels in the attic, she was certain her ankles would have twisted something awful. As it was, when her feet connected with the metal, a jarring jolt of pain radiated up through her. However, nothing felt terribly wrong. Though she was sure she'd be feeling it the next morning.

That was, if they made it to the next morning.

It wasn't like two full-grown adults landing in the back of a pickup were exactly quiet. If the gunmen hadn't already left wherever they'd been seeking cover when she'd shot at them, they'd leave soon to find them.

On cue, a man yelled from inside of the house. "They're outside!"

Suzy was whirling around, trying to get James's status on driving them away, when the engine roared to life. She barely had time to drop into a crouch and grab the side of the truck bed before the tires were kicking up dirt and rock.

The window between the cab and the back slid open just as two men ran out into the night.

"Hang on there!" James yelled through the window. The truck accelerating threw Suzy even more off balance. She slid down. More ripping sounds let her know Mara's dress was tearing again. It sure wasn't made for the field.

A familiar bang cut through the night. One of the men stood defiantly in the backyard with his gun out, but his face, as well as his aim, was becoming obscured by the distance and night. It was easy to hit a house. Not so much a moving target.

Which told Suzy these men might be familiar with guns, but they weren't pros.

"You okay?" James called. He didn't let up on the gas pedal as he took a left, putting them back on the road. Suzy was flung to the side.

"If they don't kill me, your driving might!"

Through the chaos that had turned into Suzy's evening, she heard James Callahan howl in laughter. Despite everything, it made her smile.

But it didn't last long. A pair of headlights raced onto the road behind them.

"They're following us!" she yelled.

"Might be time to get in here, then!"

Suzy eyed the window opening and did some quick math. She was a slim woman, thanks to the job and the need to stay in shape that came with it, but her part-Hispanic heritage had graced her with hips on the wide size, just like her mother. The pickup wasn't old, but it wasn't brand-spanking-new, either. Its window wasn't made for a grown woman to slide through and into the cab. Actually, it was a surprise the millionaire was driving this dinky truck rather than some sports car or hopped-up truck with a lift kit.

"I don't think I can fit," she said. "The window is too small."

James didn't turn his attention away from the windshield. The headlights were bouncing in front of them as the tires ran across the same holes that had prompted James to hold her down earlier.

"Simmons, you just jumped out of an attic vent and into a truck. You can manage this window!"

Suzy glanced over her shoulder at the approaching vehicle. It was too close. If she got stuck, then she'd be one easy target.

"There's no time!"

She pulled out her phone. She should have called the department when they were in the attic, but she hadn't wanted to give their hiding spot away.

"Here!"

Suzy turned in time to see James passing her a present.

It was a gun.

A *loaded* gun.

"You know the saying 'it's like shooting fish in a barrel'?" he asked.

"Yeah?"

James turned to give her a quick look. He was smirking.

And, boy, she couldn't stop the thought that it made him look delicious from crossing her mind.

"You're the fish in this scenario," he said. "So make sure you don't let them get near the barrel!"

Chapter Six

By the time the truck made it to the main road, Suzy had opened fire on their pursuers. She got in three shots before another was returned. It hit the top of the truck. An awful noise of metal against metal sounded above them.

"You okay?" he yelled, even though he knew she hadn't been hit.

"Just peachy!"

Two more shots came at them. Both missed. James already had his foot to the floor. At this rate, they'd be inside the town limits within minutes.

Would the men keep coming at them until their ammo ran out? Or would they stick with them until they could get the upper hand another way?

James glanced in his rearview mirror just in time to see the driver of the car thrust his arm out of his window. The passenger joined in, hand and gun sticking out of his window, too.

"Get down," James just managed to say seconds before both opened fire. One of the side windows was blown off as James ducked. The windshield followed quickly. A gust of night air pushed into the cab.

"Still with me?"

"They have more firepower! We need a better plan!" Suzy yelled back. This time there was no joke in her reply.

James cleared the glass off himself and squinted as the air made his eyes water. Suzy was right. At the rate they were going, getting into the town limits wasn't going to do them a lick of good. Not unless they had backup waiting.

They needed a better plan.

Or, at least, a different one.

"Could you hit their tires?" James yelled, already weighing the pros and cons of what he was thinking of doing.

Pro? It could get the two men and their seemingly endless amounts of ammo off their tails. Long enough, at least, to call and rendezvous with Suzy's law-enforcement brethren.

Con? It didn't work, and they were either killed by bullets or in a car accident.

James decided not to share these thoughts with the female gunslinger in the back of his truck.

"Hold on," he warned, making up his mind. "And then get ready to jump up and shoot!"

"Roger that!"

James gave her a few seconds to get a good grip. Then, with another silent prayer that he wasn't about to kill them both, he stomped on the brakes.

For the second time that night, the world around them seemed to change speed. The truck shuddered as it skidded to a halt. The glass on James and the front seat sprayed forward against the dash. The weight of a body rattled around the truck bed. He even heard Suzy yell out in surprise or pain or both. All of these things were followed closely by the horrible screeching sound of even more tires. James looked in the side mirror in time to watch the car behind them veer around the truck by what had to be inches. They rode their own set of brakes down the oncoming traffic lane before coming to a violent stop. It was a miracle they hadn't fallen into the ditch or flipped.

Now there were less than a few yards between them.

"Suz—" James started to yell. He was interrupted by a blur of fabric moving as the woman stood tall in the truck bed. All he could see was a beautiful pair of legs.

Then he was listening to the sound of her gunshots over the truck roof above him.

Three shots was all it took to deflate the back two tires of the gunmen's car.

"Hold on," he warned again. This time, as soon as he heard her drop down, James was punching the gas pedal. Instead of going past the front of their car, giving them more shots, he cut the wheel and took them the other way. Suzy might not have been chief deputy of the county they were now pointed toward, but that didn't mean James was about to risk the pair of thugs getting a good shot at her as they rode past into Riker County.

At least, James hoped the new direction wouldn't open her up to any more of their target practice.

Either way, he bet their chances were better than flashing their backsides at two men more than willing to kill them.

"You have your cell phone on you?" he asked after a minute or so had passed. Suzy was sitting up, her hair moving in the night air like she was underwater. He didn't need to be her best friend like the sheriff was to know her focus was behind them. The car and gunmen weren't following them.

But that didn't mean their friends couldn't.

Wherever the Drawler and the rest of the original group had gone, James just hoped they didn't run into them on the way to safety.

"Yeah, but it's dead." She turned so that her head was almost in the window. "Let me see yours. Because we both know it definitely works."

James couldn't help but laugh at that.

Ten minutes later and Suzy was finally done with the phone. She'd called ahead to the Calwarts County Sheriff's Department so a deputy could meet them and bring them in while another few were dispatched out to find the two gunmen behind them. She also called in to her department and put them all on alert since they had no way of knowing where the other group of men had gone. She even called in the sheriff, as best as he could tell from the snatches of yelling he heard through the wind.

By the time she had ended the call, the county road was being blocked off in front of them by two blue-and-whites. James came to a stop in front of the first car as a pair of deputies raised their guns at them.

"This is all you, *dear*," James said over his shoulder. He cut the engine and raised his hands. Before Suzy could come back with her own quip, a man stepped out of the second car. He wasn't in uniform but James could see a sheriff's badge clearly on his belt.

"Suzanne Simmons?" he called.

"That's Chief Deputy Simmons to you," she yelled back without missing a beat.

It made the man smile.

"Lower your weapons," he ordered his men. "We're dealing with family now."

James didn't get a chance to question that before the sheriff was walking through the barrier toward them. He nodded to James, who lowered his hands and popped open the door.

"You hurt back there, Simmons? We have an EMT on standby."

"I'm a little banged up but I think I'm good."

"What about you, son?"

"Nothing some Icy Hot can't handle," James answered. He got out of the truck but hung back to help Suzy out of the bed. Goodness knew she didn't need it, but that didn't stop him from wanting to offer.

"My dress wasn't so lucky," she said, raising her voice. "So unless you want to see my undergarments, Sheriff Wayland, I suggest you stop in your tracks."

Like a criminal had just drawn a gun, the sheriff reacted instantly. He turned on his heel and walked back to his men without another word. James didn't make such a retreat. Instead he took a few steps back until he was staring up at her.

"Don't worry—I've already seen that lacy

number you're trying to hide there," he defended, going around to the tailgate. He opened it and then kept his gaze high. "I'm just here to help now."

Despite what they'd gone through in the last half hour or so, Suzanne Simmons looked like she was still ready for whatever was thrown their way. Her hair was wild, her body was tense, and her dress was ruined, but she in no way looked defeated. James stripped off his jacket and held it out to her.

"This is the best I can do right now," he said, trying to coax her forward.

It worked. She dropped down on the ground next to him and wrapped the jacket around her, hiding the majority of the damage. Watching her do something as innocent as trying to cover herself with his jacket, James couldn't help but remember everything she'd just done.

It prompted an honest reaction from him. One that came out before he could censor himself.

"I don't know if anyone tells you this often enough but, Chief Deputy Simmons, you are an extraordinary woman."

Suzy lifted her chin and fixed him with a honey-filled stare. Her lips, red and plump and just asking for his, lifted at the corner.

"Don't I know it."

What the woman didn't know was James was two seconds from taking her in his arms and covering that smirk with his own, but as quickly as he had the thought, he remembered what had led them to this point.

His expression must have shown the change in feelings.

"Did you tell them about Gardner on the phone?" he asked.

If law enforcement knew that Gardner was his brother *and* had a son out there? It could jeopardize the baby even more. As well as his sister, friends and even staff. Any and all could be used to get information out of him. Not that he had much to give.

Suzy shook her head. It surprised him.

"I have a feeling that just knowing you're Gardner's brother won't make this situation any less complicated," she admitted. "I want to do as much as we can to catch those men from tonight, but if there really is a baby out there... We need to be careful and smart."

"We?"

That surprised him.

"I still don't trust you," she said, voice even. "So, I'm not leaving your side until this is finished. Got it?"

It was his turn to nod.

"Yes, ma'am."

"Good. Now let's get out of here so we can figure out what's next."

He turned to follow her but not before lowering his voice.

"How fast can you get us in the clear with these guys?"

Suzy didn't break stride.

"What? Why?"

Even as he said it, James felt a surge of adrenaline go through him.

"Because I think I know where Hank went."

THE CALWARTS COUNTY Sheriff's Department was a quick trip in Sheriff Wayland's Tahoe. Suzy had known the man for years, mostly because her father had been his friend when she was younger. Since he'd passed Suzy had kept a more professional friendship with the older man, occasionally grabbing a drink between their jurisdictions with Billy and Matt in tow.

After she'd been shot, Wayland had called, sent flowers, but hadn't visited.

He tried to make up for that in the car but Suzy assured him she'd taken no offense. Their jobs could become overwhelming at times. Not to mention busy. Like now, trying to find a swatch of armed men, barreling through possibly both of their counties while they tried to find the baby of the Alabama Boogeyman. Even thinking it made her feel insane. She'd only gone to a party and now she was a county away with a ruined dress.

Once they made it to the Calwarts department, all attempts to apologize for his self-conceived wrongdoings came to a halt. Sheriff Wayland took them into his office and buckled down on trying to get a better idea of what they were up against.

"Honestly, I couldn't tell you," Suzy said with true frustration. "I didn't get a clear picture of how many men were there, if they even were all men."

"It had to have been at least six before most of them left," James supplied. "Then we just had the two after us. Guns and ammo didn't seem to be an issue for them, either."

"And you have no idea why someone would give you an anonymous tip to go out to that house?" Wayland asked this to James directly. He shook his head.

"I wasn't aware it existed until I found the note with the address on my windshield." Suzy didn't know if she was impressed by the fact that James was weaving around stating direct lies or if it should be another point under the Reasons to Not Trust James Callahan list. Either way, she knew she couldn't hold it against him too much. Considering it had been her idea to leave the teen called Queso, Gardner, Hank and Gardner's son out of it.

Still, she wondered if that had been the right call.

"Because of my wealth I'm no stranger to the occasional prank or attempt at extortion," he continued. "Which is why I asked Chief Deputy Simmons here to accompany me since she was the only law enforcement left at the town-hall social. Though if I had realized it was more than just someone pulling my leg, I wouldn't have gone. I had no idea it was going to turn out the way it did." That last part was the unequivocal truth. On both their parts. Had Suzy had any inkling of what they were walking into, she would have trod a lot more carefully. Or at least brought more ammo.

Sheriff Wayland rubbed his chin. He looked toward the door and then to a paper on his desk.

"What is it, Sheriff?" She showed him a grin. "And don't tell me nothing because I can see it's something."

If Wayland was amused that she knew him well enough to know he was chewing on some information he wasn't sure about telling, he kept his mouth shut. Right up until James stood.

"If you don't mind, I'd like to call my sister back and make sure everything is all right."

He wasn't asking for permission, just being polite. Though he showed a small smile to her before leaving. Suzy realized as soon as he shut the door that he'd only gone so Wayland would open up to her.

Someone he trusted.

"We've heard some talk on the street about

a group attempting to weasel their way into the criminal underbelly here in the South," the sheriff led in. "Just hearsay, mind you. Sounded more like some people talking big but nothing else. But now with what happened? It would be different if it had been just the two men, but at least six with that kind of firepower?"

"Seems like overkill," Suzy supplied.

Wayland let out a long breath.

"Or a show of force."

Suzy mulled that over while Wayland checked his phone. The laugh lines at the corner of his eyes were deep. Just not being exercised tonight. Which, by estimation since her phone was dead, was technically day. She bet it was at least one in the morning.

A deep exhaustion was starting to settle the longer she sat in her chair. There were only so many jolts of adrenaline that could go through a person before draining them completely when they wore off.

"Unless there's more you need from me, I'd like to go home." She stood, not caring if he protested. "We can go give our statements and then I want to point my head toward my pillow."

Wayland looked up from his phone, seemingly lost in thought for a moment, but then he nodded. He didn't stand but motioned to the door.

"I'll keep you updated on anything we might find."

"I'll do the same," she lied. There was already a small list of details she wasn't sharing. Suzy rolled her shoulders back, trying to physically get away from the discomfort of deceit. But somewhere in her gut she felt it was the right thing to do. If they had any hope of getting to Gardner's kid before their unknown attackers could. Once law enforcement knew of James's connection to the Boogeyman it would cloud protocol. And that wasn't something they could chance with a baby out there.

Her thoughts turned to her own son.

No, she wouldn't chance their situation from going any more sideways than it already had.

"And, Suzy?"

Her hand hovered over the doorknob.

"Yeah?"

Wayland's expression was blank.

"I don't know James Callahan like you might, but I know enough to guess he's hiding something," he said, solemnly. "Be careful and try to stay out of his trouble, okay?"

Suzy nodded.

"Okay."

But she knew it was just another lie.

"What happens now?"

It was such a simple question at such a complicated time that James didn't know how to respond for a moment. Instead, he slid his phone into his pocket and took the time to really look at Suzanne Simmons.

They were outside of the Calwarts sheriff's

department, just within the glow of the outdoor lights. But it was bright enough to show him a woman who was tired and worn, but ready. The dress he'd admired from the moment he'd seen her at the party, however, had clearly seen much better days. Even with his suit jacket wrapped around her waist, one of the slits that had split farther upward was visible. Not only could he see the side of the lacy number he'd nearly died for in the attic, but the tan, smooth skin above it, too.

James focused his attention back on the woman's face. Her eyebrows were raised.

"Well?"

"Well, I think it might be time to get you out of those clothes."

Her eyebrows shot up even more. She pushed out her hip and crossed her arms over her chest. The stance did nothing to help his concentration.

"Excuse me?"

James held up his hands in defense. "We

both need to get into some different clothes," he amended. "We look like the poster couple for a zombie film."

Suzy's eyes traced the cuts he knew he had on his face and neck from the windshield's glass. He'd cleaned them up the best he could with the first-aid kit. After a good shower, he hoped they wouldn't look so severe.

"So, your plan starts with new clothes," she said after a second.

"My plan starts with getting into that." He pointed over her shoulder to a burgundy Altima.

"Whose car is it?"

James started toward it, placing his hand carefully on the small of her back to steer her along with him. Even as he moved, he felt the soreness vibrating in his legs. The jump from the attic might have hurt him more than he'd originally thought.

"Deputy Decker's."

"Deputy Decker?"

On reflex, James took her elbow as they started down the few steps between the department and the sidewalk. Her skin was as soft as it looked. Warm, too. It felt right. *She* felt right. Even in the smallest of touches.

He cleared his throat and let go. She was a distraction.

"He works here. Nice man."

James pulled out the key fob and unlocked the doors. He went for the passenger's-side door. Suzy didn't seem like the kind of woman who would let a man she didn't trust open the door for her—and James had no illusions about her still not fully trusting him—but she didn't fight it. He had to keep his gaze up as she maneuvered herself inside. However, in his peripheral vision he could still see her long bare leg when her dress parted at the movement.

"And he's just letting us take his car?"

James leaned over the passenger seat. "Of

course not. I bought it." He shut the door on her look of surprise.

Suzy kept her questions in until they were back on the main road that ran through the heart of Calwarts County. Without looking at her, he could tell she was listing off each concern and going over them all mentally before she said anything. Not only had he found she was a woman of action, he could tell now she was also a woman of contemplation. A combo that had helped make her chief deputy at a younger age than most, he was sure.

"There might be an up-and-coming gang in the area trying to establish itself," she started. "Sheriff Wayland guesses those men we ran into were a part of that group. I have to ask— did Gardner have any connections to local gangs?"

"No," James was quick to answer. "He was a gun for hire only. A floater. He liked not having ties to hold him down. He once told me the only anchor he really had to the past

was his phone calls with me." Although James
had known that as fact, saying it out loud to
someone else made the truth in it hurt. Re-
gret, anger and a growing ache of loss came
together all at once in his chest. "But I guess
that changed. Or would have, if he hadn't been
killed."

"His son," Suzy said.

James let out a deep breath. A wave of exhaustion that was in no way physical washed
away the rising emotions in his chest.

Gardner was gone, and there was nothing
James could do about that. With his brother's
death, their shared past had frozen without
hope of ever changing their future. Losing the
possibility of a different relationship was like
losing his brother all over again. Just like when
he'd heard Gardner had run away from school.

And just like when he'd found him shot to
death in the warehouse.

"It's been four months since he died," James
finally said. "If Hank has had the boy this en-

tire time, then I agree with our trigger-happy shooter from the house. Hank's waiting to do something. And considering I haven't been contacted for any reason, I'm assuming Gardner never told him who he really was. Who his family was."

"And who is this Hank?"

James rolled up to an intersection and stopped. All of the stoplights were flashing red. No other cars were on the road. It was just the two of them. He wondered if, under different circumstances, the two of them would have ever been in a similar situation. Just a man and a woman, tired in a car, making their way home together.

A different kind of ache started in his chest. He ignored it.

"Gardner, as you can guess, never really talked about his extracurricular activities with me. But sometimes he would mention an associate named Hank. On more than one occasion, he even referred to him as his friend. He never mentioned any other names, so I think it's safe to assume our trigger-happy friends are talking about the same guy."

"And you know where he is?"

James held up his finger. "I know where he likes to drink," he said. "And if you ask me, that's better than knowing where he lays his head." He pressed the gas pedal down. It felt better to do that when not under extreme duress. "Which is why we're taking a road trip tomorrow."

That got her attention. "Where? And why not now?"

"While you were giving your statement, I made a few calls. The bar is empty minus the owner, and he doesn't plan to talk until he's had some sleep." James felt his expression harden. If only for a moment. "And I want us to be smart about this. Sharp. We can't do that with the way we look and the way we feel."

Suzy's head tilted enough that he saw her hair shift over her shoulder.

"The way we feel?" Her voice was off. It prompted him to look at her. He didn't understand the change.

"Don't tell me Action Hero Simmons doesn't get tired," he said. "Because I'll be honest— I'm feeling it, and I wasn't the one being thrown around like a rag doll in the back of a pickup truck."

Suzy snorted. "Right." She cleared her throat and rolled her shoulders back. "I'd also like to reassess our situation."

"Our situation?" He glanced her way again. She didn't meet his gaze.

"I don't want to be caught in another ambush. In a dress. With only one gun."

He couldn't argue with that.

James looked at the clock. By the time they made it back to his house, he guessed it would be nearly three. What Suzy didn't know was that, even if they did sleep, he still had pieces on the figurative chessboard. Moving without him, but because of him. He'd made more than a few calls while she'd been talking to the Calwarts deputies and detective. The less he told her, the fewer reasons she had to lie when questioned. Something he was still surprised she'd done with her fellow law enforcement.

She'd kept Gardner out of it. She'd kept Queso out of it. Hell, she'd even kept the baby out of it.

James didn't know if it was because Suzy believed in him, or if it was maternal instincts coupled with experience in the field that kept her from going in guns blazing with a county of deputies behind her.

Either way, he was starting to see that, while he'd thought he knew everything about her through her reputation, she had a lot more surprises up her sleeve.

"I think the best we can do now is to head home, get some sleep and regroup later in the morning."

"And by home, do you mean mine or yours?"

The question made sense, but the way Suzy

said it brought out another feeling in James that should be reserved for the bedroom.

Lust.

That was what it was. Front and center. A feeling he couldn't deny.

But one he needed to right now.

"I wasn't going to kidnap you," he managed to joke, trying to switch gears. "But I thought it might be a good idea for you to at least clean up at my place before I take you to yours. Unless you think you can sneak around Justin before he has to get up for school."

"Don't forget my mother." A soft sigh escaped her lips. "After the accident—well, she decided it would be best to be closer to us."

"She lives with you now?"

Another sigh. "She took over Justin's bedroom. The poor kid has been bunking with me since I got back from the hospital. Though my injury…" Out of the corner of his eye, he saw her hand move to her chest. Where the bullet had hit. He remembered it in too much detail for his liking. "I don't think he realized the danger of my job until the accident. If he saw me like this?" She shook her head. "Let's just say I'll take you up on your offer."

"Good." He smiled. "Because I already had clothes for you brought to the house." Suzy whipped her head around so quickly that her hair went airborne for a split second. "Don't worry—it's not like I had them shipped in from France. I called my head of security earlier and got him to run to Walmart. He needed to get some things for Queso anyways."

"You didn't need to do that," she said. "I'll pay you back."

James slowed and then stopped at another intersection. He turned toward her and immediately fell into her eyes. They were like two pools of honey.

"Help me find my nephew, and help me find the person who ordered that his father be killed. *That's* how you can pay me back."

The chief deputy didn't miss a beat.

"You saved my life, so it's only fair that I can now help save his."

THE CALLAHAN ESTATE was surprisingly quiet. Over three thousand square feet, not including the four acres of land around it, the two-story house stood in the dark like an old friend with a welcoming hand outstretched. Suzy was surprised at the comfort she felt as they pulled up to it. Or maybe the comfort had more to do with the reaction James had to it. The moment he cut the engine, it was like he was shedding a burden from his body. His shoulders relaxed and his frown lessened as he walked with her into the house and showed her to one of the second-floor bedrooms.

"This is Chelsea's room," he said, motioning to the massive space. It seemed to double as a bedroom and a small office, though the desk was bare and most of the clothes in the open closet were gone.

"I don't want to intrude," Suzy started, taking in the various framed pictures on the walls, plastic trophies on a shelf and a few odds and ends that denoted a teenage girl had once inhabited the space. "Don't you have another two or three guest rooms?"

James waved the concern off. "None with a bathroom attached that's already stocked. Plus, she's away at college. She really won't mind. Just so long as you don't read her diary." He grinned. "Which may or may not be hidden in a shoe box beneath her bed."

James winked. "She might be good at science, but hiding things from me? Not so much." Before Suzy could really appreciate how much he clearly loved his sister, James's playful mood evaporated. "Your new clothes should be on the counter in the bathroom. There's a charger that should work for your phone in the nightstand. When you're done, I'll be in my office a few doors down. I'll leave the door open."

Suzy barely had time to thank him before

he left. Then she made a beeline for the nightstand.

Even though her mother already knew she probably wasn't going to be home until early morning, Suzy still felt a surge of panic at being reminded that her only lifeline to Justin was dead in her hands. Although, logically, she knew that her mother was more than capable of finding her without a phone—she had been married to a cop, after all, not to mention that Billy, Mara and the sheriff's department were on their family phone's speed dial in case of emergencies—finding the charger lying at the top of the drawer made her breathe a sigh of relief. She attached it to her phone and plugged it into an outlet.

Suzy rolled her shoulders back. She knew she'd been doing it all night. They were sore, just like the rest of her. She let out another long, low sigh and stalked off to the bathroom.

Like the rest of the Callahan house, the shower was impressive. Or maybe Suzy was just too excited to wash the night off herself. At any rate, the warm water was just the thing she'd been seeking. She didn't even bat an eyelash at the fact that James's head of security had taken it upon himself to buy her a bra-and-panty set, along with a plain T-shirt and pair of sweatpants. Nor did she wonder at the fact that every article of clothing fit perfectly. She made a mental note to see if this head of security would be interested in trying to find her the elusive perfect pair of jeans.

By the time she finished up in the bathroom, her phone was partially charged. She turned it on and was met with one new voice mail. It was from her mother. Suzy sat down on the edge of the bed and hit Play.

"You're lucky I got ahold of Billy and he explained your phone was dead but you're okay. I was about to hunt you down if you turned it off on purpose. Anyways, just wanted to make sure you're okay and being careful. Billy kept his darn mouth shut about what you're working on—even though you're not supposed to be working yet—so I'll trust you two. Just make sure when you *do* get your phone working to at least text me that you're okay...or else I'm sending out the hounds to find you. Love you, Suzy Q."

Suzy usually cringed at her mother's nickname for her, but after the night she'd had, she couldn't help but smile. While Cordelia Simmons moving into the house had been stressful at times, Suzy was grateful for it now. She lay down on the bed and sent a text to her mother, assuring her she was okay. She also sent a quick text to Billy, thanking him for covering for her. Suzy had only been able to tell him the bare bones of what had happened earlier—goons with guns in Riker County—before she'd had to switch gears to what was right in front of her and get off the phone. He'd promised to head back first thing in the morning.

Then she'd have to tell him what had happened.

Which made her wonder what really *had* happened. And why?

What had she gotten herself into?

Suzy took a deep breath. She still had a few questions for James Callahan.

Yet, as she compiled the ones she intended to go ask right then, the most pressing had nothing to do with the case. Instead, she found that her thoughts had strolled over into a more personal area. One that had no bearing on Gardner Todd or potential new gangs trying to make a name for themselves.

Was there someone special the millionaire had called after they'd just barely escaped death? Someone other than his sister? Someone who was just as worried as Suzy's mother had been about her?

Someone whose relationship with the man went past friendly and straight into his bedroom, only a few doors down?

Suzy closed her eyes, not liking the thought. But she was too tired to question why it really bothered her.

Chapter Seven

She felt warm.

Suzy opened her eyes slowly, trying to blink some sense into what she was seeing.

Sunlight?

"I was starting to think I might have to throw some water on you."

Suzy rolled onto her side, away from the window that was the source of her current irritation. She groaned at the movement. Pain shot through her. On reflex, she put her hand to her chest.

"What the—" she started, confused. It didn't help that James was standing next to her, looking down with a grin.

"I'm guessing you feel as great as I do," he said. "Probably worse. At least I didn't have to wear heels during most of our wild night."

The haze of sleep was clogging up her thought processes. While she was looking at James, she couldn't understand why she was horizontal and he wasn't. And why the room behind him didn't look familiar. Not to mention why she was so groggy.

Then it dawned on her.

"Oh, my God, I fell asleep!"

James's grin widened. "You sure did. Even snored a little. I thought you'd keep sleeping, too, but then you seemed to smell this." He shook a cup in his hand. The unmistakable smell of fresh coffee met her nose. It did nothing to stop the panic and heat that crawled up her neck.

"Why didn't you wake me up?" she demanded. In another move that reminded her that her body had been through the wringer, she swung her legs over the side of the bed and stood. "I have a kid! I can't just fall asleep in strange men's houses!" Suzy scrubbed a hand down her face. "Not to mention, my mom is going to kill me," she groaned. It earned a laugh from the man. Suzy shot him a look that she hoped burned.

James held his hand up to stop the next onslaught of anger she was about to let out. "Don't worry. Your mother was very under-standing when I spoke to her."

"What?" Suzy managed to ask around her pounding heart. Who needed coffee when you woke up and immediately panicked? She al-ready had more adrenaline running through her than when she'd been shot at. "You *talked* to her?"

He shrugged. "It was less me talking and more of her asking what kind of cake I like." He cracked a grin. "But I got the general point across before we started talking about the pound cake she made me while you were in recovery at the hospital."

Suzy felt her eyebrows hit her hairline.

"I told her that, after the party, I asked you to look into an issue I was having with a local company and, after some sifting through boxes of files and some light investigating, I offered you one of the guest rooms to rest in when the coffee stopped working. That's when we started talking about cakes."

Suzy's hip jutted out before she could stop it. She narrowed her eyes for a moment, then burst out laughing.

James looked alarmed. As he should have.

"You lied to my mother?" She shook her head and took the cup of coffee from him. The man might have been good at keeping his cool in danger-filled situations, but he had no idea the minefield he'd just stepped into. "And you thought being shot at was bad?"

James held up his hands in self-defense. "Hey, I figured it was either going to be me telling the fib or you. If you ask me, I took one for the team." His expression turned serious. "I've only met your mother a few times in the hospital. I don't know your relationship with her, but I know from the hospital that she seems to genuinely care about you. Which means if we told her the truth right now—"

"She would worry more than she already does," Suzy finished. "Plus, it could put her in danger. She's not the type of person to just stand by when her flock is threatened."

James gave a small smile. "So, I told the lie so you wouldn't have to. I could see how much it bothered you to lie to the deputies and sheriff last night." Like a sucker punch to the gut, Suzy felt the same guilt as before. She gave James one quick, appreciative nod. "Now, when you're ready, come downstairs. While you've been sleeping, I've been busy."

James walked to the door. Suzy set down her coffee.

"You know, it should bother you, too," she said, all trace of humor gone. "Lying, that is."

James paused in the doorway. The jokes and

charm he threw around like his own personal weapons remained in their sheaths now. His voice was cold, even.

"Sometimes lying is the only way we can protect good people." Ocean-blue eyes swallowed Suzy for a moment. The room and everything in it seemed to disappear. All that was left was the two of them—and pain. "My brother taught me that."

And then he was gone.

QUESO WAS EIGHTEEN, and had a sprained ankle and a real bone to pick with James. These were the only three facts he'd been able to get out of the boy since he'd been shown into the kitchen by Douglas, who, judging by the look on his face before he went outside, wasn't particularly happy at being saddled with watching the boy.

"You can't keep me here, old man!" Queso yelled. "I'm legally an adult! I have rights, you know!"

James finished topping off his third cup of coffee since he'd found Suzy asleep. He'd tried to sleep, as well, knowing rest was a necessity for staying sharp, but the moment his head hit his pillow he'd started thinking about Gardner. And Gardner's son. He hadn't been able to go to sleep after that.

"Yes, you have the right to be tortured and killed," James conceded. "But I think it's better for the moment that you are neither kidnapped nor dead." Queso's eyes widened enough that James knew his blunt approach had hit home. He also knew that the boy wasn't stupid. On the topic of options, he had few to none, and James didn't have the time to baby him. "Until we can figure out who this group is and why they're pulling the strings they are, you have a target on your back. One that, as I've told you, they really want to come after."

"You said that guy said that Sully wasn't dead. That he was out there somewhere," Queso tried. He put his hands on the kitchen island in the middle of the room in an attempt to really hammer his point home. "Let me go find him. He can keep me safe."

James reached into the cabinet and pulled out a mug. He kept his body turned so he could still see Queso's face as he poured coffee.

"Listen, I get it. I really do," James started. "From what I can tell, Sully saved your life, probably in more ways than one and probably before the shooting last night. I'm also going to go out on a limb and assume you don't have family to turn to, or maybe you do, and you'd rather not.

"But Sully is a smart man, despite his decision to stay on the less-than-savory side of the law. He sent you here, to me, when he could have hidden you elsewhere or even taken you with him. Not to mention, he has plenty of people who could have come to me, instead, with that address. That tells me two things." James topped off the cup and placed it on the island between them. "One, he wanted to try to keep you safe because he knows it's about to get crazy out there. Two, as of right now, he knew *this* place would be safe."

James pushed the cup of coffee closer to the boy and pointed to the cabinet behind him.

"The sugar is in there, and the creamer is in the fridge." He didn't give Queso the room to speak. Not that he looked like he knew what he wanted to say anyway. His expression was thoughtful. "You stay here, make yourself at home and let me figure out who's doing this. Okay? And then, when it's over with, I'll be happy to take you anywhere you want. Deal?"

It took him a moment, but eventually Queso took the mug. "You got until Monday," he said. "Then I'm out."

"Deal."

James took his coffee out to the patio. It was a beautiful day, all things considered. Upper eighties, low humidity and blue, blue skies. The weatherman claimed rain in the weekend forecast, but James had tunnel vision. Today was the important day.

Today he was going to find his nephew.

He took a long drink of his coffee and wondered if Suzy's willingness to bend her code by lying and withholding information to help him had anything to do with a need for revenge she wasn't telling him about. It didn't take a rocket scientist to make the jump that the people who were after Gardner's son were the same people who had hired Lester McGibbon to kill him...which, in turn, had gotten her shot. Shooting her might not have been premeditated, but her nearly dying by his hand made the blame game stretch to the same people James was after. It aligned their goals, if revenge was hers.

But was it James's goal?

Hadn't he spent months trying to find his brother's killer, even before he knew there was a baby out there?

Was *he* after revenge for his brother?

And for what had happened to Suzy?

As unwanted as they always were, images of her almost dying beneath his hands as he tried to stop the bleeding took a front-row seat in his mind.

He shouldn't have gotten her involved. The same group of men who had destroyed the small house were currently after Gardner's kid. Sure, James realized that Queso showing up at the house might have forced his hand to include Suzy in his personal investigation, but he hadn't resisted the idea as much as he could have.

The last four months had been emotionally exhausting, as he'd tried to find the right thread to pull to unravel the mystery that was his brother's life. He realized now that when Suzy had stood next to Queso, shoes in her hand and fire in her eyes, and demanded he explain everything, maybe he'd wanted to finally share everything with someone.

Or maybe just with her.

James took another drink and then sighed. The door behind him opened.

Like his thoughts had summoned her, Suzy stopped at his side.

"Whatever you've found out, you can update me in the car," she said in greeting. Pure authority rang through each syllable. Suzy might not have officially been on the job, but he bet her mind was always ready for work. "As much as I appreciate the fact that I won't be slinking home in a ruined dress and barefoot, I really want to get into my own clothes. Not to mention a holster that's more accessible."

"I don't know—watching you pull a Glock out from under your dress was quite the sight," James chimed in. "I bet it would have made the bad guys stop in their tracks."

Suzy surprised him. In one fluid motion she was in front of him, eyes narrowed and attention firmly on his face.

"I understand you use charm and humor

as weapons, so much so that I'm sure people don't even realize you're playing them," she started. "But I want you to know right now, James Callahan, that I'm not some Bates Hill resident or millionaire groupie hanging around for a show. What I am is a single mother to a boy who is still afraid of the dark and needs help with learning the right way to use a bat so he doesn't keep hitting fouls. A boy who has a deadbeat dad who never was in the picture and an overbearing grandmother who was in it too much at times. A boy who I refuse to leave behind by being careless and treating the *real* danger like it's anything but.

"So, while I can appreciate the smirks and banter and a joke or two to lighten the mood, what I need from you before we go any further is simple." She spread her fingers out and placed her hand flat against his chest.

When she spoke again, James had eyes only for her. "I need you to be on your A game, Mr.

Callahan. Plain and simple. You bring your best, and I promise you I'll bring mine."

This time there was no humor in his response. All James could feel was her hand against his chest. He wondered if she realized that four months ago he'd been doing the same to her, trying to spot her from bleeding out.

"I've always brought my best with you," he said. "I won't stop now."

Suzy searched his expression for something—he didn't know what—until she was apparently satisfied. She tapped his chest before pulling away, a smile lighting up her face.

"Good. Now let's get out of here and find your nephew."

James held up his finger to stop her from leaving.

"Speaking of being on our A game, how good are you at role-playing?"

Chapter Eight

Cordelia Simmons was short, slim and proud of everything she did. Which was never limited to and always included following her daughter around, room to room, until she got the answer she was seeking. A Southern helicopter mom, born and bred.

Among many things, how Suzy had managed to get pregnant when she was twenty-one had always been a mystery to the woman. Even when Suzy mockingly went through the logistics of how such things happened, the older Simmons put her hands on her hips and *tsk*ed at her daughter.

The moment Suzy got out of the car, wearing sweats and James's sister's flip-flops, she knew her mother would show up in spectacular fashion. Not only had Suzy returned after spending a night away from home, she'd brought company along with her. The businessman was all smiles as Suzy looked over her shoulder and told him to stay in the car.

"Do you think she'll let that happen?" he asked. With a nod, he motioned to the front of her house. Suzy didn't have to turn around to know that her mother was already on the front porch.

"If you want us to leave within the next few minutes, then I suggest you put your phone to your ear and stay put in the car," she said hurriedly, her voice low. "As far as she's concerned, I just spent the night *with* you."

A devilish look crossed James's face. It was meant to be teasing, she knew, but Suzy couldn't help but feel her body react to it. She only hoped *her* expression didn't give her away.

James responded with a smirk before pulling out his phone. It would only hold off her mother for a few minutes, at best. Which meant Suzy was already on a deadline.

She took a quick breath, pivoted and barely made it to the first porch step before her mother was all she could see.

"Honey, are you okay? Why didn't you come home last night? Are you feeling good? You look like a mess! Where's Mara's dress? Where are your shoes? You don't wear flip-flops!"

Suzy chose not to answer anything until she was inside her bedroom. That didn't stop her mother. She rattled off a few more questions before Suzy knew she'd have to bite.

"Mom, I'm okay. Like James said on the phone with you earlier, I've just been helping him with some things that he needed someone familiar with law enforcement to deal with." It wasn't a flat-out lie. Suzy just hoped her mother didn't see that it was a truth filled

with cracks. "You know how I get with some cases. A little too focused, and time slips away from me."

Suzy made it to her dresser and started to root around for undergarments *not* purchased by the head of Callahan's security. Her mother stood her ground right behind her.

"So, you sleep with James Callahan instead of coming home? And on a school night, no less!"

Suzy let out a half grunt, half sigh—a sound that only her mother could compel her to make—and rolled her eyes. She might grow older every day, but her mother could make her feel like a teen in a second flat.

"Mom, you know I didn't sleep *with* him."

The elder Simmons crossed her arms over her chest and lifted her chin. She shrugged. "Well, maybe that wouldn't be such a bad thing if you did."

"Mom!"

She shrugged again as Suzy huffed away into

her bathroom. A second later and she wouldn't have been able to shut the door. Thankfully Suzy threw the lock between them. Still, her mother wasn't perturbed.

"I'm just saying, you've definitely done worse," she called through the door. "A handsome, suave man like James? I'm just saying, he has my vote."

"Did you just say *suave*?" Suzy hedged, stripping down. "Since when do you talk like that?"

"Like what? Educated?" her mom shot back. Suzy wouldn't have done it had her mother been in plain view, but since she wasn't, Suzy smiled.

"You know what, Suzanne? I take it back. James probably deserves someone better than your ungrateful, sassy self."

Suzy felt her smile grow. Right up until the day her father had passed, he'd always said the thing he loved most about Cordelia Simmons was how feisty she could become over the smallest things. It kept life interesting, he'd say. The same opinion held true for Suzy now. While her mother wasn't always the easiest to get along with, Suzy knew she'd much rather fight with her mother than be without her.

"You need to calm down," Suzy said, half finished dressing. After hearing the plan James had hatched, she'd chosen a shirt she wouldn't normally wear out and about. For the past three years it had stayed in the back of her closet with the question of *will this fit?* hanging over it every time she'd glanced in its direction. Now she sucked in and pulled it down over her head, hoping her love of bread and pasta hadn't betrayed her.

"You're just mad because you think there's something going on between me and James, and that I'm not telling you about it," Suzy continued, voice slightly muffled as the blouse went over her mouth. She slid it the rest of the way down slowly. It wasn't until the bottom hit the waistband of her jeans that she let out a sigh of relief. Though one look in the mirror and she realized her mother was going to have a field day.

Red, sleeveless and with a neckline that plunged down into a deep V, it was a blouse made for an evening out, topped off with the rest of the night spent in. While she had a few dresses that did their job of making her feel red-hot, Suzy couldn't deny that a good pair of tight jeans coupled with this date-night blouse put them to shame. And the leather jacket she'd snagged made her feel even more slick.

She admired herself for a few seconds before applying some quick makeup and attempting to make her hair presentable. She even pulled out some perfume she saved for special occasions. It wasn't until she had her hand on the doorknob that she hesitated, wondering if her concern for how she looked was more for what she and James were about to do, or if it was more for the man himself.

Suzy took a deep breath. Then walked out to face her mama.

"Well, good gracious, Suzy Q," she started, looking her daughter up and down. "You come in wearing sweats and you leave to go clubbing? I know I said you should date him, but maybe space those dates out a little more."

"I'm still helping him with an investigation," Suzy defended herself. "And before you get all crazy, know that some of it requires some information gathering at a bar in Kipsy." She motioned to her outfit. "I don't want to spook anyone by looking like I'm a cop."

The older woman's face pinched. She frowned.

"That doesn't sound safe," she said. Her gaze flitted down to the spot on Suzy's chest that had a near-perfect circular scar. The shirt just barely covered it, but like Suzy, her mother would always know exactly where it was.

"It's important and urgent," Suzy said, not denying the situation deserved caution. "But I promise you I'll stay on my toes, keep my eyes open and be back in time to bring you and Justin supper. Okay?"

Cordelia's frown stayed put, but she nodded. Suzy gave the woman a quick hug, collected the rest of her things and was out the door and running to the car when her mother decided to get in the last word.

"Mr. Callahan, you better bring my girl back in one piece, or so help me, you'll have to answer to me!"

James leaned across the front seats and called out through the open passenger door. "Yes, ma'am!"

It wasn't until the door was shut and they were pulling away that he said anything to her.

"You definitely don't look like a cop."

There was no humor or charm lurking behind each word. No punch line he was waiting to hit. Instead, his attention was beyond the windshield, focus pulling his expression

tight. Which was good. What they were about
to do wasn't a joking matter.

THE BAR WASN'T OLD, but it carried a vintage
aesthetic that started with the wooden sign that
hung in the window and continued through the
main room with its leather chairs and wooden
bar stools, and even carried right into the men's
bathroom, where James admired the mirrors,
worn, but hanging in there.

While he scoped the restroom out, along
with a door that he assumed led to an office,
he couldn't help but get swept up in admiring
the establishment on the outskirts of the city
of Kipsy. It probably didn't help that it was
named simply The Tavern. He'd toyed with
the idea of starting up a bar while he'd been
deployed. Every idea he'd come up with had
been just as simple but elegant. He wasn't a
heavy drinker, but he'd always appreciated a
good, solid beverage.

Now, sitting in a corner of the main room,

James wished he could have a good, solid beverage other than the beer between his hands. It was for show. Mostly. He ran his fingers down the glass of his bottle, wiping away the condensation that had collected. It was his first beer, and he was doing his best to make it last. The adage "it's five o'clock somewhere" didn't feel right at ten in the morning.

"Are you sure your friend isn't trying to pull one over on us?" Suzy wasn't looking at him. Instead, her gaze was bouncing between the one wall-mounted TV over the bar that had been turned on with an old football game playing on it and the front door. Her drink wasn't as full as his. Neither was her patience. Occasionally she would bite her bottom lip. It made it harder to keep his thoughts on point. "He could be setting us up."

James started to peel the corner of his label off. He shook his head.

"She," he corrected her. "And Hale might be a lot of things, but a liar she is not. She said her contact called in a favor to get us this early meeting, assuring her friend that we weren't looking for trouble, just information. I believe her. He has no idea who we're looking for or who I am."

Suzy's eyebrow rose, but she didn't meet his eyes. Cheering blared out of the TV as a team scored a touchdown. The bartender, Rudy, who'd had to let them in and start his shift early, and had done so without comment, watched the game with little interest. He didn't watch James or Suzy at all.

"So, not only do you have a lot of contacts, but your *contacts* have a lot of contacts," she stated.

"What can I say? Everyone knows someone."

"True," she conceded. He watched as her long, thin fingers wrapped around her bottle and she took one lengthy pull. Again, James wondered what it would be like to be out with Suzy without the cloak-and-dagger, danger and deceit, and hidden guns. It was true, he'd spent the time she was in the hospital trying to get to know her when he could, but that had only resulted in polite miscommunications and then straight-up avoidance. He'd then taken to internet searches and veiled inquiries of people he knew who had grown up with her or worked alongside her. He had been curious then, just as he was curious now, about who Suzanne Simmons was outside of her job. Outside of the Riker County Sheriff's Department.

"Hale Cooper is the sister of one of my buddies from my old Air Force unit," James explained, hoping to make her feel more at ease. "Between deployments, I would tag along to some of their family get-togethers. Sometimes Chelsea was included, too. After I left the Air Force to come back here, I kept in touch with everyone, including Hale. She still comes to Chelsea's birthday parties every year." He smiled. "Basically, she's a good friend and wouldn't steer me wrong."

Suzy turned to look at him now. Her eyebrow had come back down, but he could still see a question there. One he usually got when Hale was around. "We never dated and never wanted to," he added. "It's more of a sibling bond. I would assume like the one you seem to have with our fearless sheriff." A barely-there smile crossed her lips. He'd hit the nail on the head with that observation. Not that it had been hard.

"My dad used to say that family isn't blood. It's who you decide to love and who decides to love you back. You work for it. You're not just born into it." Suzy's smile became more pronounced. James was surprised she was opening up at all. He'd only shared about Hale to ease her mind. Or maybe to let her know that he wasn't interested in his friend. At least, not in the way he was with Suzy.

The thought entered his mind so quickly that he nearly missed what she said next.

"One of the last things he ever said to me was about Billy," she continued. "He told me to look out for him because he was a good kid and he didn't have any brothers or sisters." Her smile started to fade. "I didn't know he was sick then, and trying to give me as much advice as he could, while he could, but after he passed I made sure to take what he said seriously. Though it wasn't hard. Billy's always been there, and when he couldn't be, he made sure someone was."

She snorted. It made James smile on reflex. "I got pregnant when I was twenty-one. Not ideal, but it happened. When I told Justin's father, he called me a liar and then said several very bad things. Half the school heard, because in my mind telling him at a college football game was an awesome idea, and I remember getting so sad. But then *so* mad.

He just kept saying horrible things to me. He wouldn't stop. I was two seconds from punching his lights out just to shut him up when Billy appeared out of nowhere and did it for me."

"Good man," James added, meaning it. He'd already done the math and knew Suzy had to have had Justin when she was around twenty, but beyond that he hadn't known what had happened for sure. Especially not with Justin's father.

"Yeah, I can't deny it was really nice to have him shut up, but—" She held up her index finger. "The real moment I knew Billy had become my family for life was just after that, when Justin's dad left town. I hadn't had the guts to tell my mom yet, and my sister was out of state, so there was no buffer.

"I was sitting on the front porch, trying to get the nerve up, when Billy shows up in his dad's Bronco. I remember being so scared about the future, about being a mom, and a single one, at that. And there he was, goofy as hell with a smile to match. He walked up and just said 'You two are going to be fine.' Just like that. No lie, just confidence. He believed it so much that it was enough at that moment to help me believe it, too." She shrugged. "He's been Uncle Billy ever since."

Suzy's affectionate demeanor shifted so suddenly that James tensed. There was ice in her words as she spoke.

"Which is why we need to figure everything out before he gets back into town," she said. "I don't want to lie to him. Not after everything he's done for me."

James wanted to assure Suzy that he'd do everything in his power to make sure it all worked out, but the moment he opened his mouth to do so, a man walked into the bar. He nodded to the bartender, who immediately stood up and left.

The man didn't look their way until Rudy was out of the room.

Then the man walked toward them with purpose.

Chapter Nine

The man, burly and tall, bald and bearded, pulled a chair over and sat down heavily. He wore a dark shirt and dark jeans, and had tattoos across the skin that showed. Suzy estimated his age around upper forties. She didn't recognize him, and by the look on James's face, neither did he. However, he got right to the point, which Suzy appreciated.

"So, you have a question for me. What is it?"

Suzy wanted to adjust her stance so she could more easily get to the gun hidden beneath her jacket. It was an urge she had to tamp down, however. The point of their cover story was to hide the fact that she was law enforcement for as long as they could. They didn't want to spook the man if he wasn't on the good side of the law. And if he had any affiliation with Hank or Gardner, it was safe to assume he wasn't.

James kept playing with the label from his beer. He seemed so relaxed. A cool cucumber.

"We're looking for a man named Hank," James said. "A mutual friend told me and my girl here that we could trust him."

The man didn't give anything away. His expression remained the same one of slight annoyance that he'd shown them the moment he walked in.

"I'm sure there are a lot of Hanks in the world," he answered. "What makes you think I know where this one is?"

James motioned to the bar on the other side of the room. "Because that same friend told me this is where he likes to drink, and since you own the place, I'm betting you already know who I'm talking about."

"Even if I did know who this Hank was, you haven't given me a reason to tell you," the man countered. "What's your business with him?"

"My business is my own," James replied. Suzy was impressed at the level tone, as if he were calmly telling a child no instead of refusing to answer a man twice his size.

"Meeting with you was a favor given to an associate, but I'm telling you now you're *in* my business. You can't make demands and expect me to buckle to them."

He crossed his arms over his chest. Suzy saw a new set of tattoos on the back of his arm. A snake with stripes coiled near his elbow. Although unique and adventurous, the rest of his tattoos were the standard macho variety. No gang-related symbols jumped out at her. The bar owner was tough, but if he was on the seedier side of the law, he didn't broadcast it in body art like some of the men and women the sheriff's department had handled in the past.

"I'm not trying to be disrespectful," James

said. "It's just a personal matter we'd like to keep quiet. So why don't you name your price, instead. Payment for your information."

James didn't make a show of taking out his checkbook, like they did in movies. It was the best move to make, in Suzy's opinion. He was exuding nothing but confidence in his nonchalance. No fear or worry.

The man, however, was unimpressed.

"Money isn't a motivation to me. I don't know you *or* your lady. And I don't think any mutual friend of ours is going to change that fact, especially if it has to do with one of the people who may or may not be a patron of my bar."

He rose in one quick movement. James didn't flinch. Suzy's fingers itched for her gun's trigger. If the man was holding a weapon, it was well hidden. He took a few steps away from them and held his hand out to the door. "You can tell me right now who you are, who your friend is and what you want with Hank if you find him. Even with a pretty lady on your arm, I'm not a man who takes payoffs."

The urgency that Suzy had been feeling all morning finally came to a head. There was a child out there who was being targeted for whatever reason, and James and Suzy were on a short list of those who wanted to keep him safe. She felt the slithering shame of having already lied to those in law enforcement who would also try to keep the boy safe, and she'd simply had enough. James opened his mouth, but she stood and spoke first.

"Gardner Todd wanted us to meet Hank," she said. "And to be really honest with you, we're pressed for time. So instead of acting big and bad, actually talking to us would be preferred. We need to know where Hank is. Now."

Suzy couldn't read his reaction. He now looked mildly bored instead of annoyed. Still, his tone fell flat.

"Gardner Todd is dead," he said simply. "And

has been for months. Whatever business you think you had with him died with him. It has no place here."

"Don't you want to know who we are?" Suzy prodded.

He shook his head. "No, I don't. The favor was to meet you and I've done that. Now see yourself out. The beers are on me."

"Listen here, buddy," Suzy started, finger going up to stop him from talking over her. But instead of hearing authority in her voice, all she could hear was her mother. "We need to—"

"Did you ask anyone else to come meet us?"

Suzy and the man turned to James. He was on his feet, staring past them. For a second she thought the question was for her. Then the man answered.

"No. I'm assuming you didn't, either?"

Suzy heard a car door shut before she pivoted to look out of the front window. James swore loudly. The SUV didn't have bullet holes in it, but it was identical to the vehicle that Suzy and James had been chased by the night before. Three men got out. They were dressed in jeans and T-shirts. If they had guns—which, if it *was* the same people, she assumed they did—they were most likely concealed in the backs of their waistbands.

"No. They're not with us. But if it's the same people we ran into last night, then I'm betting they're here for Hank, too," she answered. "And I guarantee they won't ask you to talk like we did." She didn't recognize any of the men, but then again, she hadn't been able to make out any faces the night before. But she couldn't be certain if the same was true for the men. She *had* been in plain view during the chase and the following shoot-out.

"Just in case you don't know them, I'll tell you those aren't good men," James warned. His hand slid around hers. He started to pull her toward the back hallway. "It might be best that we leave while we can."

Suzy thought about standing their ground, testing their cover of boyfriend and girlfriend and seeing what happened next, but then the men stopped in their tracks and looked back at their car. Inside, the bar fell silent. James's hand tightened slightly. It was warm and reassuring. The men looked like they were waiting for something. Suzy didn't like it.

Neither did her gut.

"I'm calling in backup," she said, making a decision. Waiting to see if something bad was going to happen wasn't a strategy they should be using anymore. Not after what had already happened. She felt James stiffen, but he didn't argue. She glanced up to see his focus was on the bar owner. His arms were still down at his sides. If he drew a weapon, she'd be faster.

"You're cops?" he asked, voice low.

"I am," Suzy retorted, dropping James's hand and going for her gun. The bar's front windows were heavily tinted. It was easy for them to see out, but those in the parking lot would have a harder time making heads or tails of the people inside. Still, she felt exposed. She didn't like it.

Out of the corner of her eye, she saw James straighten his back even more. The men in the parking lot were still looking at their car. Suzy pulled her phone out with her free hand.

"I'm not a cop," he announced. "I'm James Callahan, Gardner Todd's little brother." Suzy couldn't help but turn at that, surprised. James's jaw was set. Hard. His focus was on the man in the middle of the room. "And I'm pretty sure you're Hank." He pointed out of the window. "Which means they're here for my nephew, and I'm not going to let them get him. What about you?"

Suzy had several questions—how had James known the man was Hank? *Was* he really Hank? How had the men in the SUV found them? But it didn't matter. The bar owner only had one.

"What was Gardner's real name?"

James didn't miss a beat. "Trick question. Gardner *was* his real name. He was named after our grandfather on our mother's side. All he did was drop the Callahan after he ran away."

Suzy held her breath, waiting for a reaction from the man at James's answer. Finally she got one. Now she could read his expression with ease.

Relief.

"He told me he was going to talk to his brother about the kid, but he refused to give me a name. He was more uptight about privacy than I was."

"Where is he?" James pressed. "The boy."

The bang of another car door shutting prevented an answer. All three turned to watch as a fourth man stood next to the SUV.

This time it was Hank who swore.

"Who are they?" Suzy had to ask.

The men came together and began their walk across the parking lot toward the front door.

Whoever the fourth man was, he had changed the group's demeanor. They weren't there for a leisurely drink or two. They weren't there to ask questions politely. They were there for answers.

And blood.

A sentiment Hank already seemed privy to.

"Follow me," he said quickly, swinging around and rushing to the back hallway. Suzy hesitated. James didn't. He had her hand again, fingers gripping hers and the phone in her hand. She let herself be pulled along as she realized that Hank was projecting another heavy emotion.

Worry.

"I don't know the first three, but the last fella is Grayton McKenzie," Hank called over his shoulder. Instead of leading them to the back door, he swung a right and headed through a fairly large but cluttered room.

The kitchen.

The bartender looked up from the sandwich

he was eating. One look at Hank and he was as rigid as a soldier before a commanding officer.

"Rudy, I need you to go to the house and check on Patricia. Bring your gun." Suzy opened her mouth, but Hank was faster. "He's got a permit for it and no criminal record. But I need you to go with him and go ahead and send deputies out there. An ambulance, too."

"What? Why?" James was just as lost as she was.

"There are only two people who knew how to find me. Grayton landing on my doorstep means he either found me through Gardner or through my wife. If it was Patricia, then you'll need to get to my place fast. My lady plays by the rules, but she's a fighter, too. If Grayton and his boys went asking questions, she didn't give them answers easy." Rage and worry battled for position across his face. So did sincerity. He looked at James. "That's where your nephew is."

James's grip tightened around her hand. As

if a current of electricity was running between them, she felt a charge of excitement. Excitement and caution.

"You're not coming with us?" she asked, trying to ignore the surge of adrenaline beginning to move through her.

Hank shook his head. "Grayton isn't the type of man to stop unless he's gotten what he wants. I want to find out what that is."

"You're outmanned," Suzy pointed out. She nodded back behind them. On cue, the antique bell James had admired over the front door sounded. "If we stay, there's a better chance of—"

"You make sure my wife and that boy are okay," he interrupted. "I'll deal with Grayton."

The two men looked at each other. Finally, James nodded.

"Hello?" a man called from the front room. "Can we get some service in here or what?"

"Now go," Hank said to Rudy.

He was wide-eyed but accommodating. He

went to a door on the opposite wall and opened it, revealing the back alley.

"Hold your damn horses," Hank called out, already moving back into the hallway. "I'm comin'!"

"They could kill him," Suzy whispered, but James didn't pause. He pulled her along with him all the way until they were in Rudy's truck. Even then, he didn't let go of her hand until they were racing away from the bar.

HANK'S HOUSE WAS in the country, just like Gardner's had been. However, it was less off the beaten path and seemed more lived-in at first glance—garden beds in the yard, patio furniture on the front porch and even a wreath on the door. James knew that judging people based on their appearances wasn't always reliable, but he couldn't help but be surprised that the man they'd left at the bar lived in such a quaint place. There was even a little gnome wearing a flowered dress next to the mailbox.

Then again, according to Hank, he didn't live alone.

"Patricia is a really nice woman. I hope nothing bad went down here," Rudy said, breaking his silence. He'd kept his mouth shut as Suzy had spent the ride in the back seat on the phone with the sheriff's department. He hadn't even muttered a word when she'd called local police to The Tavern, making sure the officers knew that Hank was friendly but also a person of interest. James wanted to ask if Rudy had known Gardner, but he knew it wasn't the time. Suzy and the bartender weren't the only ones with guns. He had his compact .45 caliber in the holster at the back of his pants and wasn't afraid to draw if he needed to.

"It doesn't look like anyone is here," James said.

Rudy stopped his truck a few feet from the closed garage door. There were no other vehicles in the long driveway or on either side of the house. There was a house in the distance, but it was one heck of a walk. James squinted but couldn't make out any vehicles that way, either. If any of Grayton's pals were around, they were hiding well enough.

"Rudy, have you ever been inside?" James asked after Suzy hung up with whoever was on the phone. Rudy put the truck in Park but didn't cut the engine. "Do you know the layout of the house? Any good spots where someone might try to jump out and get us from?"

The man sucked on his teeth, brow furrowed. "The living room is right when you walk in, and there's a small hallway to the left with a bedroom and a bathroom. I've never been to their bedroom upstairs," Rudy answered. "Only time I've ever been here was at a Christmas thing Patricia threw last year. I got plastered, and they let me sleep it off in the room downstairs. The kitchen's in the back with a door that goes to a patio. I think there's a shed behind the garage, but I was too wasted to really check it out at the party."

Suzy slid forward in her seat. Her service weapon was already out. She might not have been cleared for field duty yet, but James knew from the determination shining bright and clear in her eyes that not even the sheriff could have stopped her.

"Is Patricia the type of woman to take us out with a shotgun if she thinks we're a threat?" she asked.

Rudy hesitated, then nodded. "She'll protect herself, and if there's a kid in there, she'll protect him, too."

"Does she know you well enough that she'll believe you when you tell her we're friendly?"

Rudy didn't hesitate this time when he nodded.

"Hank doesn't have a lot of people he trusts, but I'm one of them." His chest puffed out in pride.

"Okay, leave the truck running but come with us. Keep your gun in its holster until I tell you to bring it out. Or we start taking fire,"

Suzy ordered. She shared a look with James. It was worried. "The closest patrol to us is a few minutes out. An ambulance is just behind them. But if there's a chance there's a hurt woman and kid in there?"

James understood. And agreed.

"Right behind you, Chief Deputy."

Chapter Ten

"Hey, Patricia, if you got a shot on us, don't take it! Hank sent us to make sure you're okay!"

Rudy yelled the same line three times before they made it to the front door. So far, she hadn't responded. No one had. It wasn't until they were smack-dab in front of the door that the sense of something being terribly wrong crept in. It wasn't locked, but it had been. The dead bolt hung in its intended spot, but the wood around it was splintered.

The door had been kicked in.

James turned to Suzy. She made a succession of hand motions that made him feel like he was back in boot camp again. She wanted him to go right while she went left when they went inside.

No dice, he thought.

"We stay together," he mouthed.

The urgency of the situation didn't give Suzy room to argue.

"Stay here," she whispered to Rudy, instead. "Keep an eye out."

The bartender nodded, hand hovering over the spot where his gun must have been hidden in the back of his pants. He might have originally seemed as big and bad as his employer, but James could see how unsettled he was. Nervous and not ready. Which meant he probably didn't find himself in this situation often.

Suzy led the way into the house, gun sweeping the room seconds before James did the same. Together they pivoted, ducked and moved through the living room, hallway and two guest bedrooms like synchronized dancers. Their flow never wavered as they scanned each room in silence.

James balanced being alert with being observant. *Southern Living* magazines were spread around almost every room alongside football paraphernalia and a few issues of *Jeeps* magazine. Fresh flowers were in worn vases in both bedrooms, while the bathroom was pristine. Both beds were made, the rooms they were in smelling as pretty as the flora around them. Yet, despite the bottom floor being pristine, there was one detail that made the unease in James's stomach heavier. However, he kept it behind closed lips as he led Suzy up the stairs to the one part of the house Rudy had never seen.

The master bedroom was small but, like the house itself, quaint. It was furnished with white linens embroidered with flowers and leaves, and an oversize leather chair in the corner with a quilt across it. A large window let in enough sun to warm the space. Again, not what James had expected from Hank, not in the least. Not that anything he'd learned in the past two days had been less surprising.

The master bathroom was pretty much the same as the bathroom downstairs, and both closets in the bedroom were filled with women's and men's clothing. One had a small box in the corner of it. Suzy popped open the lid to confirm it contained nothing having to do with a secret baby.

Once they finished, Suzy lowered her gun.

"Someone broke the front door to get in, but there are no signs of a fight." She motioned around the room. "And unless we're missing something pretty big, I don't think any baby lives here, or any older kids, for that matter. Do you think Hank was playing us?"

James shook his head. "I think Patricia *was* here. I noticed that there are no bags in this entire house." Suzy's eyebrow rose. He elaborated. "In the closet downstairs, under the beds, the cabinets...no duffel bags or luggage.

Not even Walmart bags in the kitchen. Someone who is *this* neat with their house, and this organized, could easily handle fleeing with a kid without leaving any traces behind. I'm guessing it was Patricia. There are easily thirty issues of *Southern Living* magazine throughout this house, and every single one is neat and orderly."

"Suggesting Patricia wouldn't get sloppy if she needed to stay discreet," Suzy said. "Like if she needed to leave in a hurry with a baby no one is supposed to know about."

James nodded. He walked to the window and looked out into the distance. The driveway started at the end of a long, thin road that branched off an even longer county road. Both were in clear view.

"She could have gotten lucky and seen a car or two on the county road, and gotten ready just in case," he ventured. "If she saw them turn, then she could have had two minutes, maybe, to do something."

"But do what? Grab a baby and a bag with all of his belongings and then…hide? Run?"

James snapped his fingers. "Rudy said there was a shed out back," he said, suddenly remembering.

Suzy pulled her gun back out, and together they hurried to the backyard. By the time they were pushing wide the shed's door, which was hanging open, but not broken like the front door, the faint sound of sirens began in the distance.

And James was cussing up a storm.

"Or maybe Hank *did* play us," he snarled, moving out into the grass. Like the house, the shed didn't hold a woman or baby or anything out of the ordinary. "Maybe he's working *with* that Grayton guy. And I just gave him my name." He turned and kicked the side of the shed hard. Frustration raged through him in sync with the painful throb that shot through his foot. He didn't care.

"But someone *did* break in the front door,"

Suzy pointed out. "And, even though we don't know much about Hank, he seemed genuine in his concern for his wife."

James felt the anger in his words before they even came out. "Gardner was good at a lot of things, but he was *great* at lying. Who's to say his friend isn't just as good?"

Suzy was in front of him in a flash. She put away her gun and furrowed her brow. Her proximity sent a jolt through him. It was alarming, but not in a bad way.

"Get it together," she ordered him. "I know there's a lot going on, but we need to keep our heads on straight. Second-guessing yourself and the gut feeling you must have had about trusting Hank is going to get us nowhere. And it's *my* gut feeling that we aren't following a bad lead." Her voice softened. "So, if you can't trust yourself, can you at least trust me?"

It seemed like such a simple question. Could he trust Suzanne Simmons?

James already knew the answer.

Yes, he could.

The real question was, could she trust him?

He opened his mouth to ask it when movement over her shoulder caught his attention. Rudy walked through the back door and pointed past the two of them.

"They're going to the wrong house!" he yelled.

James and Suzy turned in unison. The county road curved around Hank's house and went alongside the house he'd noticed in the distance. A field of grass and a few trees were all that stood between the backyard they were currently in and the side yard of the other house.

"Maybe Patricia *did* have time to get out of the house," Suzy said, excitement making her words come fast. "She just didn't have a car to leave in, so—"

"She fled on foot. If she was fast enough and they went into the house first, there's a chance they wouldn't have seen her," he said. "I bet she made a run for the neighbors'!"

APRIL DONAVAN HAD been tending to some sod her son had laid the day before when she'd been startled by her neighbor running toward her, a bag on her shoulder and a baby in her arms.

"I know Patricia," she said now, nearly out of breath from the excitement. It probably didn't help that Suzy and James were two of many people bustling around her yard. The deputy she'd called was talking to the deputies Suzy had called, while the EMTs were packing up to leave. "Her and Hank have lived there for about a year, and both are really kindly— which at first I wasn't so sure of considering how, well, how—" She motioned to her arms.

"How *decorated* Hank is," James supplied. April nodded quickly, clearly relieved she didn't have to talk about his tattoos.

"But they've been over to eat a few times and I've been there, too, and they're just really nice folks, you know?"

"And in all that time you never saw any sign of a baby," Suzy clarified.

"No! Not even once!" April flung her arms out toward Hank's house in the distance. She shook them, all dramatics. "The first time I saw that baby boy was when Patricia was running at me, hollering about needing the keys."

This was the second time they'd heard the story since they'd gotten Rudy to drive them across the field. The local PD and some of Riker County's deputies had been directed to look for Patricia and the baby in the surrounding areas, while law enforcement on the scene was waiting for the next senior person to give orders. Since *technically* Suzy wasn't on duty yet.

"I didn't even get a chance to answer her before she was running inside and grabbing my keys off the hook," April continued, voice going higher and higher. "Then she yelled at me to get inside, lock the doors and call all of you! What's going on? Whose baby was that? Where's Hank?"

"That's what we're going to try to find out," Suzy said, turning on the soothing tone she used on Justin when he was upset. She reached out and squeezed the older woman's arm to try to reassure her with contact. "You did the right thing in listening to her and calling us out here immediately." Suzy nodded to one of the deputies from the department. Her name was Maria, and she had a natural way of keeping people calm in not-so-calm situations. At seeing Suzy's nod, she smiled wide. "Why don't you let Deputy Medina talk to you about what happens now?"

The crease across April's forehead lessened as she caught Maria's eye. She nodded and moved away, already recounting how crazy the afternoon had been to the deputy before she'd even gotten near Maria.

Suzy let out a sigh. The heaviness that only frustration could bring felt like it was pushing her down, trying to wear her out before she could finish the case. She couldn't deny she'd missed the feeling a little. Four months in recovery without working to search out justice had started to make her feel antsy, restless. Now? Well, one look at James and she wished the sense of purpose that washed over her at being a part of an active case wasn't at his expense.

He hadn't left her side since Hank's house, and he hadn't said a word since April had finished telling the first round of her story. Suzy knew it wasn't him giving up or being afraid. He wasn't the kind of man to give up so easily. Yet it was as if he was his own island, standing in the middle of a storm. Resilient. Mysterious.

Alone.

And, just like that, Suzy was consumed with the need to join him on that island. To brave the storm and help him navigate it.

Before she could voice any part of the feeling, though, her cell phone vibrated. Another sigh escaped her.

"Simmons," she answered.

It was Matt. He didn't waste any time with formalities.

"Suzy, The Tavern is a bloodbath over here," he jumped in. "Two dead and one unconscious and being transported to the hospital. Didn't you say there were supposed to be two more people? We're only counting four total."

James must have read the alarm in her expression. His brow furrowed.

"Yes, the owner plus the four men." Suzy hesitated. "Unless Hank's one of the deceased or hurt." James's eyebrows dipped even lower. "He's bald with a lot of tattoos."

A pause. "No, no bald men here."

Suzy's stomach dropped. "What about a man with black hair, shaved close to the scalp? Hank called him Grayton McKenzie?"

This time there was no pause. *"Grayton McKenzie?"* The sound of movement filled her ear. Then Matt was whispering. "Suzy, I don't know what you're in the middle of, but I think it's time we all had a talk. Grayton McKenzie isn't just your run-of-the-mill bad guy. He plays dirty, and if he's linked to what happened to you and James Callahan, then things only stand to get dirtier."

Suzy's stomach had already reached the ground. Now it was digging a hole to jump into.

RUDY HAD NO idea where Hank might have run off to—not that they knew if he'd done his disappearing act voluntarily or not. And on the off chance he had, Rudy certainly wasn't saying. Suzy watched from the front porch as Matt did what he did best: get someone to talk. Yet, through all the questions and answers, she believed Rudy was telling the truth.

He had no idea where Hank was or how to get hold of him. The same went for Patricia.

And James's nephew.

The millionaire had detached from her side as they'd gone back to Hank's house to meet with Matt. Even if Suzy had kept things informal between herself and James, Matt stuck to the book and wouldn't show the crime-scene pictures from the bar until James stepped away. Which he did without fuss, much to her surprise. He didn't even try to turn on his charm, not that it would have worked on Riker County's lead detective.

"The best I can guess right now is this guy here was shot from the front *and* the back, so I'm guessing he was caught in cross fire." He pointed to one of the three men who had gotten out of the SUV before Grayton. He was face down on the floor, next to the bar. Matt switched the picture to the second victim. Another man from the SUV. This one's neck was at an angle that made Suzy's stomach twist. "As for this guy, his neck is broken. No other injuries. Which meant he either let it happen or it was an opening move. A surprising one, at that."

"Geez," Suzy said with a low whistle. "And to think we were worried Hank was out-manned."

"Yeah, no kidding." Matt changed the picture again. This one was of a man on a gurney. "He had a gunshot to the stomach and was rushed into surgery. We're running his face now. Hopefully we'll get a hit soon."

"And Grayton McKenzie?" She hated to ask the question she already knew the answer to, especially since the name alone evoked an undeniable tension in the detective.

Matt rubbed the back of his neck and filled his chest with a deep breath. When he let it out, there was less worry in it and more anger. "I'm about to go talk to Captain Jones, who's become more familiar with him and where he might go than I am, but honestly, he hasn't been *seen* in a few months. In fact, the only person that *I* knew who had the juice to get him out…" In his voice was guilt, anger and a longing to change the past. All three created a shadow across his expression. It was a look she'd seen on him in the hospital after she had woken up from surgery. She'd tried to explain several times that he didn't need to react that way when he looked at her. He'd done nothing wrong.

"Let me guess." Suzy lowered her voice, careful with talking about the dead. Especially now that she knew his brother. "Our one man was Gardner Todd."

"Yeah," Matt confirmed. "His life was a mystery, but his death?"

Suzy put her hands on her hips and sighed. "Even more questions."

"And some I need to go ahead and start working on." Much like she'd done with April, Matt reached out and patted her arm. Working at the sheriff's department was more than a job to them. It was friendships and family. When one of them hurt, they all hurt. He gave her two good pats and then excused himself. He disappeared into the house, writing pad already out. The beginnings of a stress headache started to build between Suzy's eyes. She wanted a lot of things at that moment. Answers. A hug from her son. Coffee.

"Suzy."

The voice came from behind her. She could be blindfolded, drunk, half-asleep or buried in a box and she'd recognize that voice. Velvet smooth.

"James," she returned. Soon he was standing in front of her. All worry. All handsome.

"We need to get back to my place." He said it with enough force that she believed that need. Her mind jumped gears. Suddenly she was thinking about her own needs. Ones that twisted sheets and made her knees weak.

"We need to go back to the bar and grab your car," she said instead. "And then I need to—"

"I just got off the phone with Sheriff Reed,"

he interrupted. "We need to go to my house because he's already there."

"Billy's at your house?" she asked, confused. She hadn't talked to him yet. "I didn't even know he was back in town. Why is he at your house?"

James was all stone.

"Because we need to talk."

Chapter Eleven

Billy Reed was standing on the back patio, surveying the acreage with his hands in his pockets, wearing his cowboy hat on his head and his sheriff's badge on his hip. Suzy approached him with nerves in her chest and shame in her belly.

The last time she'd talked to him, she'd withheld information—important information—about Gardner Todd's child and the connection they both had with James. If there was already a nasty group of men willing to kill to try to get the baby *without* knowing his uncle was a millionaire and one of the most influential men in their county, then filling in the blanks for the public only would put the boy in more danger. Still, Suzy had lied to a man she trusted completely, and there were no two ways about it. She'd lied to her best friend. Not to mention her boss.

But would she do it again?

Once Billy knew about who Gardner *really* was, then all eyes would go to James. His life would never be the same. Even his sister and nephew would become subject to the prying eyes of an entire county. Not to mention the men and women who might try to seek out some kind of revenge on him as payback for Gardner's criminal activities.

This wasn't just about her loyalty to Billy or her department. She had to make a choice, right then and there. Loyalty or…

Suzy hesitated in her steps.

Never did she ever think she'd be where she was, trying to decide between Billy and the department and a man she barely knew. Yet that was exactly what she was doing.

And it was eating her up.

Especially when she realized her heart was betraying itself and leaning away from her makeshift family toward one she wasn't even a part of. Toward a man she couldn't trust.

Billy glanced over his shoulder but didn't turn around. Suzy came to a stop at his side. Her stomach was in knots. He spoke before she could make up her mind.

"So, James is Gardner Todd's little brother, huh? Can't say I saw that one coming." Suzy's mouth fell open, surprised. Billy took a deep breath and let it out slowly. He didn't seem as confused as she was.

He didn't seem confused at all.

"But why do they want Gardner's son if they never found out the connection to James and the Callahan fortune?" He turned, brow lined with contemplation. "Where's the boy's mother?"

Suzy's shock was replaced by his line of questioning, specifically the last one.

"No one knows how the mother is, though..."
Heat crawled up Suzy's neck. It held shame
and anger. "I realize now that we never asked
Hank that question. We were so focused on
Gardner and finding the boy, and then the men
showed up."

Billy shook his head. "And that's another
thing—Grayton McKenzie making moves all
of a sudden? Very *public* ones, at that?" He
took his hat off and rested it against his chest.
"I knew Gardner's murder would have reper-
cussions beyond what law enforcement might
see, but this? I sure picked a fine time to go
out of town, didn't I?"

"Yet you're already caught up?" Suzy ventured. No one at the department knew the specifics, and she sure hadn't told anyone.

Billy's index finger started to tap a rhythm
against the brim of his hat. It was a thinking gesture he'd made since he'd been elected
as sheriff. He was beyond contemplative, and
Suzy couldn't tell what he was feeling. Thank-

fully, she never had to wait long with him. He always told her. Which made her feel all the more guilty about her recent silence on everything that had been happening.

"James," he said simply. "He called me while you were talking to Matt at Hank's place. Said he needed to tell me something he had begged you to keep quiet about before either one of you knew how big this thing was. That he was Gardner's kin and the grand prize all of your new buddies have been shooting for is his nephew. Matt had already looped me in that Grayton was involved. I was also told there's someone named after cheese dip taking refuge here by James's invitation." He shrugged. "All in all, it makes sense not to let the cat out of the bag about the Callahans, so I thought it best we make a more strategic move and have a meeting here. Gotta say, I don't mind the view."

His eyes roamed over the trees and grass out in the distance. Billy Reed was a country boy at heart. He could spend hours admiring something others might have taken in in a glance. He was the type of man who took the time to appreciate his surroundings, and Suzy couldn't help but feel pride that he seemed to like James's home.

It was a thought that surprised Suzy. But she didn't have time to question it.

"I'll tell you one thing for certain, though," he continued, a small smile pulling up the corner of his lips. "Riker County is never boring."

He wouldn't get an argument from her. "You got that right, Sheriff."

To prove his point, Billy's phone chirped out some music.

"Mara," he announced after looking at the ID. "I can already hear her worry without even answering the phone."

Suzy couldn't help but laugh. While Mara would always worry about her husband, it never detracted from her strength. It was another reason Suzy felt close to the woman.

Mara had been through her own trials and tribulations, and fought her way back to standing. She even had the scars to prove it. Still, Suzy could sense the worry before he answered.

"Then right now probably wouldn't be the best time to tell her that the dress she loaned me... Well, let's just say I won't be getting my deposit back."

Billy shook his head, still smiling. "I'll save that conversation for you to have with her later."

Suzy patted him on the shoulder. "Good man."

He excused himself and, walking onto the grass, took the call from his wife. Suzy wanted to take advantage of the interruption, so she hurried back into the house, thoughts picking up speed in tandem with her pace. James had gone to his office and it was there she found him, standing behind the desk, brow furrowed.

"You called Billy," she rushed, forgoing any attempt at beating around the bush. "You voluntarily told him about everything. Why? Now your family is vulnerable."

His eyebrow rose and ice-blue eyes found hers.

"If anything, *hiding* my family's past has made us vulnerable. Something I will do my damnedest to make right." His fist balled next to an open box on the desktop. "Telling the sheriff was the right thing to do."

A surge of insecurity pushed past Suzy's lips before she could understand where it was coming from. "You didn't trust me."

James gave her a questioning look. "I didn't trust you with what?" he asked, head tilting slightly to the side.

Suzy's heart started to beat faster. Her stomach started to flutter. She didn't understand what her body was trying to tell her mind. So she spoke without thought.

"You didn't trust me to see this through, to catch Gardner's killer and save your nephew," she said in a rush. "You decided you needed Billy's help more than mine."

Her cheeks burned as soon as the words left her mouth. What was she talking about? Billy was her boss—her family—and here she was, hurt that James had gone over her head? It didn't make sense. Suzy opened her mouth to try to take it back, try to cover up the feeling of vulnerability that must have shown on her face, but nothing came out.

James's expression turned sharp. He came around the desk and stopped close enough that she could smell his cologne. Or maybe it was his soap, still lingering across his skin. Waiting to pull her in.

The heat in Suzy's cheeks traveled south. Her heartbeat was all-out galloping.

"Telling him was never about not trusting you," James said, keeping his voice low. "I decided to do it because I didn't want you to have to keep lying for me. For my family. I don't want anyone else hurt because of me or mine. Especially not you."

The racing, the fluttering, the storm of emotions. They all slowed.

"You told your secret so I wouldn't have to lie to Billy." She spelled it out, to make sure she understood. "But you don't know me."

James's frown smoothed out into a smirk. "I know enough."

The rush of emotions and thoughts inside of her abated.

Her picture from earlier, of James as an island in the middle of the sea, shifted. Instead, she realized he was the man in the eye of the storm.

And she'd just broken through the clouds.

In two long steps, Suzy closed the space between them and, with less thought than it took to walk to him, she pressed her lips to his.

James didn't reciprocate as she moved into the kiss.

She didn't need him to.

All she wanted to do in that moment was to show him how much she appreciated what he'd done. From saving her life to telling a truth that could hurt him so she wouldn't have to tell a lie, he'd been more than good to a woman who had given him nothing but grief and suspicion throughout the past four months.

Suzy might have felt more comfortable shooting out of the back of a truck than expressing her feelings, but right then, it was the best she could do.

She ended the kiss as abruptly as she'd initiated it.

The man was no longer smiling.

"Sorry," she said, taking a step back. "I just—"

James slid his hand across the skin of her neck beneath her ear and then fisted it in her hair. He used the contact to pull her back to him. His other hand fastened on her hip, and she could feel the warmth of his hand through the thin fabric of her shirt.

Where her kiss had been impulsive, his kiss was intense.

Hot and powerful. Crushing and consuming.

He deepened the kiss by parting her lips with his tongue. It was a shock she realized was pleasant. Her body reacted of its own accord and leaned up and against him, wanting more. Needing more. She gasped into him as he pressed against her. His body also wanted hers—another pleasant realization as she wound her arms around his neck. He wasn't the only one who wanted to be closer.

Yet, in the blink of an eye, James broke the kiss.

And untangled himself.

"I'm sorry," he said, voice full of grit. "I can't."

A different kind of heat roasted Suzy's skin. Embarrassment? Disappointment? She didn't have a chance to dissect the full body blush that he no doubt could see. Without another word, James Callahan left his own office.

Suzy leaned on the desk. No matter the reasons behind either one of their moves, she couldn't deny one thing.

It had been one hell of a kiss.

She inhaled long and deep and then let it out slow and steady. The open box on top of the desk caught her eye. Needing a distraction, she peered inside. Stacks of pictures created a mountain. They were old, definitely from a disposable camera. At first glance she could see they were scenes of several strangers doing what people normally did in pictures. Standing in front of a Christmas tree. At a park. Playing in the snow. Laughing by a pool.

However, the one that sat on top of them all seemed to be the most important.

It only showed two people, standing with their arms around each other and smiling for all they were worth.

A teen and preteen.

A big brother and his little brother.

Gardner and James Callahan. Before life decided to show them how temperamental it could really be.

"WE MIGHT HAVE a lot of questions, but that's good, because that means we also have a lot of pieces, too."

James, Suzy and Billy stood around the kitchen island with determination, purpose and mugs of coffee. Suzy had swept into the room just after Billy finished making a phone call and, after James quickly filled the sheriff in on some specifics he hadn't had time to give on the phone, she was rallying their spirits.

"And having a lot of pieces is better than having none," she finished.

It was a simple observation, but it did the trick. James felt himself stand straighter and puff out his chest. Yet maybe the boost had less to do with her narrative and more to do with what had just happened to them upstairs.

Kissing Chief Deputy Suzanne Simmons was something he'd thought about, sure, but he hadn't counted on the feelings that had attached themselves to the act. The urge, the want, the need. It was like he'd been put under a spell.

He'd wanted more, and then he'd remembered why that was a bad idea.

He would soon become a target, if he wasn't already. Not only of Grayton McKenzie, but the general public. While Gardner had been a silent part of the criminal underworld in Alabama, there were still plenty of upstanding people who had known his name. Keeping his association from them and law enforcement had had a cost.

One he didn't want Suzy to pay.

Now he needed to focus.

And not on how the woman across from him had tasted.

"Okay, so, let's start making those pieces fit," James said. His voice came out a little too low. He compensated by clearing his throat. Suzy's eyebrow rose enough to let him know she'd noticed, but the sheriff started without hesitation.

"Gardner leaves his son with his friend Hank, who may look big and bad but his record is clean save for a few drunken fights back in the eighties, and goes to meet you to tell you something. Presumably that he has a son and you have a nephew." James nodded. "Lester McGibbon, a man who had no reason to kill, shoots Gardner in the warehouse."

"And then Lester shoots me," Suzy said matter-of-factly. "And James shoots him and he's declared dead on scene. His identity is kept under wraps for a week while the department and local PD try to get a hold on what might happen when the news of Gardner's death hits the streets."

James motioned to Suzy and then himself. "We go to the hospital, and while you're in surgery, I call my family attorney for an alibi so no one will find out Gardner's my brother." James paused, needing to explain further. "He's a good man and I tried not to lie to him, but I didn't want to put Chelsea in any danger from the blowback of the news getting out. But I also didn't know about the baby then. I would have done it differently had I known. My attorney chalks my going without him to look at a property up to my being impulsive and doesn't question it further. Oh, and, by the way, I own the warehouse now, if that can help us at all."

Billy nodded. Suzy looked surprised but nodded, too.

"For the next four months, I use every connection I have to try to figure out why Lester did what he did, until I come to the conclusion that he was hired to do it or maybe forced," he continued. "That eventually leads me to the name of a man who deals in information, using less-than-legal methods."

"Sully the Butcher," Billy said. While they'd been on the phone earlier, the sheriff had confirmed he knew of Sully, though he'd never had a reason to deal with him personally *or* professionally. Sully tended to stay north of

Riker County and almost always under the radar.

"He met with me yesterday morning and agreed to try to find out who had ordered the hit on Gardner, but *without* resorting to violence. I knew he could get to the seedier parts of the criminal outfit around here easier than I ever could. I figured it would be safer for everyone that way." James shifted his gaze away from Suzy. While he had believed then what he said, a part of him now wondered if he'd gone to law enforcement in the first place instead, if he'd be sitting with his nephew right now.

"And then one of Sully's protégés shows up at the party last night with an address for you from his boss," Suzy said, picking up where he left off. "Someone ambushes Sully and his men, wounding Sully in the process, and then we take the address and go to a house in the country. A house that you guess belonged to Gardner."

"Men show up, armed to the teeth, and are told to go find Hank and Gardner's son," Billy said, taking over. "James tracks down Hank at a bar he used to hear Gardner talk about, and you two have a chat with him. He identifies Grayton, tells you where the baby is, and we find out that his wife had fled with the boy. Two of Grayton's men are found dead at the bar, one is in surgery now, and both Grayton and Hank are missing."

They shared looks with one another all around.

That was it. The whole story. No more lies or omissions.

"So, those are our pieces," James said.

"And there are some questions we need to answer before we can see that puzzle," Suzy jumped in. She ticked off each one on her fingers. "Where did Patricia go? Did Hank and Grayton leave the bar together? How did Sully get Gardner's address?" She hesitated before putting up her fourth finger. "And if Hank *is* with Grayton and knows who we are, what does that mean for us if he shares that information?"

That question hung heavy in the air.

Then crashed into the ground as someone screamed outside.

Chapter Twelve

James was the fastest. He'd bolted out of the kitchen before Suzy had time to step clear of the island. Billy was next. The aches from the night before came back with force as she followed, but she pushed through them.

A woman had screamed.

Had Patricia learned about James already and come to deliver the baby? Had she been followed? Were Grayton and his men on the front lawn, guns up and high as they stood next to the garden beds?

The possibilities had her breathing ratcheted up higher than when she'd been shooting out of the back of a pickup truck.

Was the baby out there, too? Right in the middle of harm's way?

Suzy shut down all lines of *what if* the moment she ran through the front door.

There were no droves of men with guns pointed at them. Nor were there any babies caught defenseless between them. Instead, there was only Queso, standing with his hands straight up in the air, a cigarette hanging limp between his lips, James's and Billy's guns both pointed at him and a girl clutching her purse to her chest.

"Chelsea?" James asked, clearly surprised. He wasn't the only one.

"What in God's name is going on around here?" she shrieked. "Why do you have a gun?"

James holstered the object in question. Suzy followed suit. Billy stayed firm in his stance.

"Why did you scream?" James replied, matching her volume.

She pointed to Queso, who wasn't moving

an inch. "I dropped my phone and bent down to get it, and then saw *this* guy just staring!"

James turned so fast on Queso that it was nearly comical.

"You were staring at my sister while she was bending over?" he asked, volume still high.

The poor boy tried to sound tough, but his words lost their edge around the butt of his cigarette.

"No way, Padre! I was going crazy inside, so I wanted to take a smoke break." He pointed at Chelsea, hands still in the air. "It ain't my fault she didn't hear me walk up. I wasn't checking her out, just trying to figure out who she was!"

James's anger wasn't appeased so easily. Suzy walked over to his side and touched his elbow lightly. Then she nodded to Billy. He lowered his gun.

"This is just another reason not to smoke," she said, reaching out and taking the cigarette from his mouth. He made a face like he was going to complain, but she gave him a look she often used on Justin when he needed to think before he spoke. Suzy went to the sidewalk and ground it out. "Come clean this up and get back inside," she said. "I've got some more questions for you." No one complained at the order, and although Queso looked like he wanted to, the boy dropped his arms and complied.

Not before casting a dirty look at Chelsea, though. She returned it in kind.

"What are you doing here?" James said, rounding back to her when Queso was inside. "Why aren't you at school?"

"You told me not to come home!"

James waved his arms around wildly. *"So you came home?"*

The girl nodded with fervor. "Of course I did! You've never told me not to come home, so I figured something was wrong!"

"That makes no sense, Chels," he shot back.

"Well, I was right, wasn't I?" She pointed to Billy and Suzy. "Unless you're always ready with backup to come out, guns blazing, and I've just missed it all these years."

James dragged a hand down his face.

"I'm going to go ahead and try to find out as much as I can about Patricia." Billy jumped in, looking at Suzy. "Tell me if your talk with Queso brings anything new up. I'll put Matt and the captain on the rest. Keep your phone on you and let me know." He reached out to shake James's hand, then tipped his hat to Chelsea. "Take care."

Billy paused at Suzy's side. "I'm going to arrange for a unit to keep an eye on the estate entrance," he said, voice low so the others couldn't hear. "Still, stay on alert."

"Yessir."

They watched as Billy got into his Bronco. It wasn't until his engine turned over that Chelsea's confusion soured into concern.

"What's happening, James? What's wrong?"

James let out a sigh. He glanced at Suzy. She knew what he was feeling. While Chelsea was his little sister, she was also like his daughter, in a way. The age difference plus the fact that he'd raised her made him a man caught between brotherly affection and paternal love. He wanted to protect her, but now he had to figure out how to do that. It was something Suzy couldn't help him with. Especially since she had no clue if Chelsea knew who Gardner Todd even was.

Suzy's heart clenched for the man who had rejected her not fifteen minutes before.

It was an odd sensation. One she decided not to dwell on.

"Why don't we go inside first," she suggested. "It's a little too hot out here for my tastes." Suzy smiled and held out her hand. "My name's Suzy. We've never formally met."

Recognition flared instantly behind Chelsea's baby blues. Seeing the two Callahans standing next to each other, Suzy couldn't deny the resemblance between them. They had matching dark hair—although Chelsea's was more styled than James's was—and clear blue eyes, and they even shared the same chin. Suzy had seen a picture or two of their mother in the house and saw that the female Callahan had inherited the matriarch's petite stature. If there was any of their father in her, Suzy wouldn't know. She hadn't noticed any pictures of him in the house.

Chelsea was staring at her intently. "As in Chief Deputy Simmons?"

Suzy was surprised but nodded.

"In the flesh."

A small smile picked up the corner of Chelsea's lips. Her gaze flitted to her brother, then zipped back.

"I'm glad to see you out and about." Her gaze jumped down for a second to Suzy's chest. Then her smile widened. "James has told me a lot about you."

It was Suzy's turn to smile. "Hopefully all good things."

"Are you saying there are bad things about

you I should know?" James chimed in. It was his way of trying to lighten the mood, she knew, but it still sent a thrill through her.

She shouldn't have kissed him. Not with everything going on. Not without knowing if the chemistry between them was something James Callahan could have with anyone he wanted.

Suzy knew that the kiss had been a mistake. He knew that, too.

But knowing something was true and accepting it as such were two completely different things.

THREE HOURS PASSED and no one had learned a thing.

Well, except for Chelsea. She'd found out she was an aunt and that her nephew was still missing. Apart from that, everyone attempting to find him had come up with nothing but dead ends. But not for lack of trying.

James looked down at his cell phone. He'd made so many calls that it was hot to the touch.

The well of contacts he'd used the first time to ferret out information about Gardner had dried up with the disappearance of Sully. Not even Queso could find someone who knew if he was still alive, let alone where he was. James couldn't help but feel sorry for the boy. Sully might not have been the best role model, but it was clear to James now that he was all the boy had.

Once again James came back to his nephew. And worry and guilt were immediately replaced with anger.

Why had Gardner waited to tell him?

Why hadn't he set up a better contingency plan?

Why hadn't Gardner listened to him all those years ago?

"Knock, knock."

James lifted his head. Suzy stood in the doorway. She was frowning.

"I think it's time I went home."

Another simple statement that had a strong

effect on him. But it wasn't unexpected. They'd been together for almost twenty-four hours.

"I'm sure you want to see Justin."

She nodded. "I do. But I won't stop working on this. I'll work from home."

James waved a hand, dismissing the thought.

"You've already done more than enough, plus there's more people on it now. The sheriff's department included."

Suzy nodded again. But she still wasn't smiling. "I know it's not my business, but how did Chelsea take the news?"

James looked over her shoulder to the closed bedroom door. Suzy took a step closer so he could lower his voice.

"She's a tough cookie, but I threw her a curveball," he admitted. "One of many." He sighed. "There's a thirteen-year age difference between us. Sixteen years between her and Gardner. She was only a few months old when he ran away. By the time she could understand what a brother even was, he'd been scrubbed out of the family by my father. I honestly don't even know if he would have ever told her Gardner existed if it wasn't for me and my mother. Even then, it was something you just didn't talk about with the old man in the room."

James rubbed the back of his neck. Talking about his family wasn't one of his favorite things to do. Especially about his father and the divide he'd created. "Either way, I didn't like her not knowing him, and so I told her about the Gardner I'd grown up with when she was old enough. Not the one who'd earned the title of Alabama Boogeyman. I was trying to protect her. Trying to protect him, too. The Gardner that was still good, the one I was proud to call my brother."

James fought the urge to ball his hands into fists. Suzy had asked a simple question and here he was, again, regaling her with the epic dysfunction that was what it meant to be a Callahan.

"By the time she was old enough to want anything more than just stories from me, my father died," he continued. "It wasn't until I left the Air Force and became her guardian that we had to have a more serious talk about him. I wanted to be honest with her, since it was just the two of us. I wanted her to know what it was like to be trusted and loved by a parent, even if I was her brother. I don't think she knows how to process the idea of a baby Gardner out there when she barely knew how to process *Gardner* being out in the world but not a part of our lives before he was killed." He couldn't help but smirk at how much he'd divulged. "I guess I could have just said that from the start."

"It's only fair, since I talked your ear off this morning," she replied without missing a beat. "Sometimes you just have to say what you're feeling."

"True."

A few seconds of silence stretched between

them. James thought about Suzy and the bed behind him. He wanted Suzy. There was no doubt about that now. But he also wanted to keep her safe.

She'd already nearly died because of his family's baggage.

So, instead of pulling her in for a kiss he hoped she'd never forget, he said good-night.

"Sleep well, Chief Deputy," he added before she turned away. "You've more than earned it."

She flashed a quick smile. It looked as tired as he felt. Wary, even. Then she was gone.

James looked back down at his phone.

It was still warm in his palm.

A WAITING GAME. That was all it was now. And she wasn't happy about it. Patience wasn't her strong suit.

Aggression was.

Someone rapped on the door. It took all the calm she had left not to shoot through it. Especially when it was Grayton who peeked his head around it.

"I was wondering when you'd slink back here," she greeted him with a snarl. "Next time maybe I should send someone younger. Or maybe I should just do it myself. Heavens knows good help *is* hard to find."

Grayton tucked his chin but held her gaze. It was the only form of pushback she'd gotten from him in the last year. The only resistance he attempted. The rest of her cronies didn't dare even that much.

"We underestimated him. Hank," he tried. At least his voice was submissive enough. She loosened her shoulders. "He killed Lee and Ryan. Rocko is in the hospital."

"I know," she said. "I always know, remember? Your merry band isn't the only group I have on the payroll."

She adjusted the pearls around her neck until the clasp was at the nape. She was overdressed in comparison now that Grayton was there.

His suit was covered in blood. No bullet holes but more than a few slashes. He had certainly fought his way out of the bar, all right.

Not that she cared.

He'd had one job, and he hadn't delivered.

Maybe he picked up on that thought. His eyes shifted from her for a split second before slinking right back.

"Then I guess you know that his house is crawling with cops right now."

"I do." She leaned over and rested her elbows on the desktop. "Old news may be news, but it's not something I like to deal in. Impress me or, my God, Mr. McKenzie, at least try. I'd hate to have to change our arrangement."

Instead of letting her threat make him squirm, he tried to stand taller.

"I didn't want to come back empty-handed. So I didn't." He took a step forward and looked very much like a man pretending to relax because he was on more solid ground. However, he'd been around long enough to know that solid ground didn't exist in their business. At least, not hers.

You either did well or you didn't.

And she didn't have patience for those who didn't.

"After Hank took off, I figured he'd run home to see about his woman," he continued. "The cops were already there. Deputies from the county, too. I recognized one of the detectives from a few years back who helped take out that dimwit who tried to take over Bryan Copeland's old drug business. He was talking to a woman. I'm pretty sure it was the same one who shot at us at Gardner's place. She got into a car with another man. And guess where they went?" He grinned.

She raised her eyebrow, knowing there was a fifty-fifty chance he was going to disappoint her with his answer. "Where?"

"That fancy house out in Bates Hill. The mansion."

That got her attention. She felt her brow furrow.

"Do you mean James Callahan's estate?"

Grayton nodded with fervor.

"Well, that *is* interesting. What does the Bates Hill Savior have to do with Gardner?"

While she was pleasantly surprised with the information that Grayton had brought her, she didn't expect him to answer that. He kept silent as she stood and walked around the desk. Her heels tapped out a soothing rhythm against the hardwood.

Soothing to her, anyway. Grayton couldn't hide the muscle in his jaw that jumped. It made her feel even more powerful. She sidled up to him and flashed a smile she hoped chilled his blood.

"I guess I'll just have to go and ask him myself," she cooed into his ear. "After all, isn't the old clichéd adage something about if you want anything done you should just do it yourself?"

That clearly surprised him. She had a front-row view of his eyebrows bunching in together. She liked the reaction. Those who stuck to routines never flourished. It was about time she changed her tactics from a behind-the-scenes style to a more visible one, out in the field.

"Now, Grayton." She brought her hand up and cupped the side of his face, turning it so their eyes met. "While I'm away, why don't you go get yourself cleaned up?"

He gave one precise nod.

Unlike her other minions, Grayton knew when to keep his mouth shut. It was done more out of fear than strategy, but she appreciated unquestioning loyalty.

Hot and pure anger heated beneath her skin.

Loyalty.

She didn't take betrayal lightly.

Before he could flinch at the change in her expression, she grabbed both sides of his cheeks and squeezed until his lips puckered.

It wasn't until her nails bit into his skin that she spoke.

"After that, you're going to figure out who that woman was and why she's interfering with *my* business. Got it?" She nodded his head for him. Droplets of blood oozed out onto her once-perfect manicure. She applied another wave of pressure until he couldn't stop from wincing. She smiled and loosened her grip. He didn't move a muscle as she stroked the half-moon marks across his skin.

"Good," she cooed again. "Good boy. Because I really *do* like you, Grayton. I'd hate to have to deal with replacing you, especially when we're so close. But don't think I won't, if needed. I'm not above eliminating those who disappoint me."

She wiped the tops of her nails on his shirt and patted his chest. While she kept her smile in place, she knew neither one of them believed it held any mercy.

"Just ask Gardner."

Chapter Thirteen

James might have had more than enough money to hire a personal chef, but he wasn't about to deny the world his famous breakfast for dinner.

He stood in front of the stove and slung eggs into a pan while keeping his eyes on the bacon. Chelsea manned her usual post next to the waffle iron. Looking at her, now nineteen years old, he couldn't help but see the preteen he'd taught how to use it.

"So, you never finished telling me," he started. "I know you aced your lab, but what grade did you get on your final history project?"

After hearing the news that Gardner's son

was just out of their reach and they'd been all but ordered by the sheriff to stay put, Chelsea had been quiet. That wasn't unusual for her personality. She'd always been more of a contemplative kid. While some people barely thought about the words before they came out of their mouths, Chelsea often overthought hers. Sometimes, if you paid close enough attention, you could almost see her picking the words in her head, careful to use the right ones.

It had worried James, at first. Coming home to raise a sister who was only ten had been enough to send him diving into the pages of countless parenting books, but it had been Chelsea's quiet and reserved personality that caused him to stress. That was, until he realized that listening more than speaking wasn't a bad trait, just different from how he and his brother had behaved. And their father, when he was around, had been the louder parent. It hadn't mattered who was right if no one could hear the other points being made.

James had felt right at home with the drill sergeants in boot camp.

"It wasn't as good as my biology lab, but it wasn't as bad as I thought it would be." She poured batter over the waffle iron.

"Are we talking low A or high B? Or are we more into the Cs?"

Chelsea's contemplative nature also came with a dose of perfectionism. While she was willing to slack when it came to chores or summer jobs, her grades were important to her. Doing poorly on a test, in her mind, was the equivalent of doing great to most other people.

"High B, *but* I could have done better." She huffed and brought down the top of the iron. "I blame that stupid guy I got partnered up with. He was more interested in talking about himself than in helping me. I should have done the entire thing myself, but all I could hear was you in my head." She cleared her throat and adopted a baritone. "'Doing someone else's work usually only hurts them in the long run, Chels. Especially if someone is trying to take advantage of your work ethic.'"

James threw his head back and laughed. "That goes double for talkative, self-involved college boys."

"Oh, don't worry. I already told him all about my big brother who did two tours in Iraq. Which is why I think he never bothered me *outside* of the library."

"That's my girl."

James finished scrambling the eggs and turned his attention to the bacon. This was something he couldn't deny he missed. The house seemed so much bigger when Chelsea was gone.

His thoughts reverted to Suzy. It had felt nice having her around the last two days. Even when she'd been sleeping in the other room, James had felt an odd peace start to settle, just knowing she was there. Throughout his time in Bates Hill, he'd dated a few women he'd considered introducing to Chelsea. Yet he'd never noticed their absence the way he did with the chief deputy.

They'd been through a lot of near-death situations. With the baby missing, a potential new gang rising and a man who could disappear as easily as Gardner could, stakes were high. Anyone could get caught up in the moment. Maybe that was all their kiss had meant.

Maybe without danger and bullets, their interest in each other wouldn't exist.

James didn't like that thought. Nor the one that came next.

With or without Suzy, his future was going to change. Because of Gardner's son.

What was the point of having the money he did and spending years networking for connections when he couldn't use them to help find his own flesh and blood? Shouldn't *some-*

one be finding something by now? Statistics alone should have been on their side.

"Will it be like this when we find him?"

James paused, spatula in midair. Apparently Chelsea's thoughts had found their way onto the same wavelength.

"What do you mean?"

She took her time in responding, choosing her words carefully again, no doubt. Slowly she opened the iron and forked out her waffle. Then she was ready.

"Gardner's son. Our nephew. Will you raise him by yourself, too, here in the house, like you did with me?"

James looked over at her. She kept her eyes on the new cup of batter she was pouring into the waffle iron. There was guilt in the question. He knew it, because he'd heard it before. No matter how hard he had tried, he couldn't seem to fully convince her that, sure, leaving the Air Force had been hard, but it was nothing compared to what abandoning her would have been like.

Just like if he abandoned his nephew.

"Of course I will," he answered honestly. "But I won't be alone." He hoped she heard the smile in his voice. "You're going to be on diaper duty as soon as you step through the front door when you come back from college. Plus, I've already decided that after teaching *you* how to drive, I'm done with that forever. I've been in combat zones less terrifying."

"Hey! That's not fair." Her normal voice returned. "I wasn't that bad!"

"You weren't that good, either," he mumbled.

She laughed. "I heard that."

The weight that had settled on her shoulders seemed to lift a little. James was glad for it. While, technically, she was an adult, he didn't want her to bear the particular burden that came with being mixed up in Gardner's criminal life. They'd agreed years ago that they'd protect her from it, and James would be damned if he didn't keep trying. She was still trying to find her place in the world; she didn't need to be caught in a web of constant worry, too.

They finished each of their cooking duties and settled around the table in the eating nook. It wasn't until she spoke that he noticed she'd made an extra waffle. Which made her next topic of conversation no surprise to him.

"So, I know you said that he needed to keep a low profile and he helped get some information for you about Gardner, but—" she dropped her voice "—is his name really Queso? Don't get me wrong, I love a good dip, but that's a little intense. And kind of ridiculous."

James snorted and then sobered. He couldn't help but picture the scene the night before, when a blood-soaked boy had limped into the house yet was only worried about his boss. His friend. Despite his rough-and-tumble persona, Queso had been a better guest than most.

He wasn't about to make fun of the boy now,

especially when they didn't know what he'd been through. The ridiculous nickname might be covering up a pain that neither one of them could understand.

James decided to set the tone for Chelsea so she knew exactly where he stood on the boy.

"That's what he's comfortable being called. And we'll respect that until he tells us otherwise." James was stern enough to leave an impression. Chelsea nodded and dropped her gaze to her food. She danced her fork across her waffle. He eyed the extra one off to the side and sighed through a smile.

"I guess it wouldn't hurt to ask him to come eat with us," he said, standing.

"You make it sound like you think we're too good for him," she noted with her own smile. But it zipped right off a second later. Her eyes widened. "Or maybe *he* thinks he's too good for us?"

James couldn't help but laugh. Always concerned, that was Chelsea Callahan's natural state.

He mussed her hair as he walked past, earning a swat or two from her. "Probably a little of both," he answered. "But I guess it wouldn't hurt to try to get him socialized. I'd hate for him to miss out on my famous breakfast for dinner."

Queso had been given the run of the house, true to James's word. Instead of staying in the living room, glued to the TV, he'd surprised James by hanging out in the small library at the corner of the first floor. When James had been house hunting, privacy had been the number one desire on his list. It was the main reason he'd bought such a big house when there were only two of them to live in it. However, the library had definitely been the second reason he'd signed the papers. Built-in bookshelves lined two of the walls, while a large window that looked out into the backyard took up the third. James had done some of his best business thinking in that room.

Queso sat on the couch by the window. His head was bent over an open book. Whatever it was, he was halfway through it. Another surprise.

"Want your mind to be blown by the best bacon and waffles you ever had?" James asked in greeting. The boy jumped and slammed his book shut. Then he went on the offensive.

"You shouldn't just sneak up on people like that, Padre. Wear a bell or something."

James shrugged. "It's not considered sneaking if it's your house. I think it's just called walking then."

Queso snorted. It lacked any real humor, though. "I don't think I can consider this a house," he sneered. "It's got more rooms than a motel."

James shrugged again. He knew he lived in what most considered a mansion, and that he was lucky for it, but he'd tried to keep everything inside its walls simple and modest. He had money, yes, but he never flaunted it or took it for granted. All he ever wanted to do with it was help people.

Queso threw the book on the cushion next to him and scooped up his phone. No one had called him since he'd shown up the night before. It was clear that that was eating at him. James guessed the rising anger coming off him wasn't meant for him at all.

"And how can you joke around and just stuff your face when that kid is out there? Is it a rich thing to not care? Don't you want to find him?"

James had expected the question. It didn't lessen the sting.

"Running around like chickens with our heads cut off isn't going to help anyone. Not *the kid* and not Sully, either." Queso's jaw tightened. "It would be different if there weren't people out there looking, but for us, the best thing we can do right now is calm down, take a beat and be ready for anything. Sarcasm and a hunger strike aren't going to get either one of us what we want."

Queso didn't look swayed by James's points. His expression had frozen in a sneer.

"At the very least, come and thank Chelsea," James added, when Queso didn't appear to be getting up anytime soon. "She already made you a waffle."

"She made *me* a waffle?" he repeated.

The sneer was replaced by interest, interest James realized he didn't like. Before he could pepper in a small speech about what was appropriate in terms of interactions with his little sister, a sound he truly didn't expect echoed through the house.

The doorbell.

He was so caught off guard by it that he froze to listen as the series of chimes played out a song.

"I'm guessing by your face that you didn't

invite anyone over for that famous bacon of yours?"

James didn't answer. He pulled his phone out from his pocket. No missed calls or texts. The landline hadn't rung, either. If anyone wanted to come over they were supposed to call. Not to mention, there was a deputy patrol at the entrance of the estate. They weren't supposed to let anyone past until authorized by the sheriff or him.

"Stay here," James ordered, not liking how his gut twisted.

Queso didn't listen. He trailed behind James through the back hallway that led across the bottom floor and into the living room. A set of double glass doors separated it from the grand entryway.

"Queso, you need to hang back," James said, pausing before he opened the doors. "I can't keep you safe if everyone knows you're here."

"Who do you think's at the door, Padre?"

Queso asked with a smirk. "Bad guys don't ring the doorbell."

James rolled his eyes. "Just get out of sight for a second," he said in a rush. "And keep quiet."

The doorbell chimed again. Fortunately, Queso listened. When he was out of the living room, James swung the glass doors wide and walked into the entryway, body already tense. He didn't know what he expected when he opened the door, but it surely wasn't who he found himself staring at.

Tall, slim and wrapped in a white pantsuit, a woman James had never met before was smiling at him. Her lipstick was bloodred, complementing the dark auburn hair that fell to the tops of her shoulders, and she had a large, expensive-looking purse at her side. He placed her age at around his.

What he couldn't place was one single reason why she would be standing on his doorstep.

"Mr. Callahan," she greeted him. "I'm so sorry to intrude, but I was wondering if I could have a moment of your time?"

Chapter Fourteen

The popcorn had burned, but Justin hadn't complained. He'd eaten almost all of it during the movie. Now the bowl was empty in his lap, a book open on top of it. Suzy had already gone over all his homework due Monday, while her mother had excused herself to take a bubble bath.

If routine held, she'd be out by the time Justin was winding down for bed. The three of them would talk until it was time for lights-out, and then Suzy's mother would fix a glass of warm milk and question her daughter about work and potential suitors before recapping what had happened on the latest TV show or book she'd occupied herself with that day.

This was their normal. The way the Simmonses operated.

This was where Suzy was comfortable.

Or had been comfortable, at least.

Now?

Now she finally had someone to talk to her mother about when she brought up men. Not that she would. When it came to James Callahan, Suzy realized he was the embodiment of a wild card. And after he'd broken their kiss earlier, he'd all but shuffled her back into the deck.

Which was for the best.

She didn't need to be giving in to any impulses, especially ones involving the millionaire.

Suzy sighed. She left her phone on the arm of her chair and stood. She was between phone calls with Billy and Matt and anyone else she could think of who might be able to help track

Hank, Patricia or Gardner's son. No luck. It was like everyone involved had vanished into thin air.

Her heart felt heavy for James.

Impulses aside, he was just a man scrambling to save his family, and that in itself pulled at her heartstrings.

One look at Justin with his hair tousled, dark cheeks lined with freckles and round, chocolate eyes focused on his book, and Suzy couldn't imagine how desperate she would feel if she couldn't find him.

Justin raised his head, feeling her "mom stare," as he called it.

"Mom. You're staring. Again."

That annoyed tone that kids seemed to pull out of thin air laced his words. Suzy also couldn't imagine Justin as a teen. She wondered how James had handled that phase with Chelsea.

There she was again. All thoughts seemed to lead back to the man now.

"I'm just wondering how you managed to do this." She bent over to grab a few stray kernels that had found their way under the coffee table. "You know this stuff is supposed to go into your mouth, right?" she teased. "Maybe I should get one of those horse feeders and strap it around your head."

"Then you have to get Mimi one," he said matter-of-factly. "She dropped those!"

Suzy laughed, picturing her mother being just as messy, and put her hand out for the bowl. He gave it up but followed her into the kitchen.

"Mimi was worried about you today," he said, still using what he clearly thought sounded like an adult tone. "She called Aunt Mara and talked for a while about it."

Suzy felt a flutter of guilt, but she didn't show it.

"And you know this because Mimi told you?" she ventured.

Justin looked sheepish. "I heard her."

"You heard her as in you were eavesdropping, or you heard her as in you picked up the other phone and listened that way?" It was a trap. One that he'd been snared in before. Either way, he knew the outcome was trouble. Still, he surprised her by answering.

"I picked up the phone in the living room to listen," he admitted. Then added in a rush, "But I thought it was you! And I didn't listen to a lot of it."

She crossed her arms over her chest and narrowed her eyes a fraction. Honesty was the best policy, but she'd trimmed the truth when it came to explaining why she hadn't come home the night before. Justin knew she was working and that she was with James—a man he'd met at the hospital and said he liked—but she'd told him that it was nothing for him to worry about.

He *was* only ten, after all.

"We've talked about this before," she reminded him. "You don't spy on people unless you're getting paid to do it as part of a profession. And even that sounds a little uncool."

He dropped his gaze, but Suzy knew it wasn't just his curiosity that had prompted him to do something he knew would get him into trouble. He'd been worried, too. And he still was.

Suzy relaxed her posture and opened the pantry. There was only one thing to help ease his mind. Or, at least, distract it. Standing on her tiptoes, she reached to the middle of the top shelf.

"Next time—" She jumped up, trying to grab the box, but missed. "Next time you are worried—" She jumped up again. This time her fingers wrapped around the edge of the box she was aiming for. She pulled it out. Justin's eyes were wide when she turned back to him, box fully in view. "—just talk to me or Mimi. You can even call Aunt Mara if you need to. Okay? No more of this sneaking around."

He nodded, but his eyes stayed on the box. Like he was in a trance.

"Can I have one?" He clearly couldn't hold himself back from asking.

This wasn't exactly part of their routine, but she figured it might take his mind off everything. At least for a little bit.

"As long as we can eat them before your grandma comes out," she said, dropping her voice to a whisper. Her grin was matched by her son's.

Suzy opened the box of sugar-filled, pre-wrapped honey buns—their little secret treat that Cordelia Simmons had forbidden—and threw one to Justin. No sooner had he caught it, though, than the sound of shuffling slippers filtered from the hallway that led to the bedrooms.

"Hide them," Justin whispered, panicked.

A giddy excitement filled Suzy's stomach. She didn't have time to throw the box back onto the top shelf of the pantry, so she threw it in the other direction. Justin laughed as it soared over his head and hit the top of the dining room table on the other side of the kitchen cabinet. There was no way her mother hadn't heard that, but it was worth a guaranteed nagging in Suzy's future to hear a carefree laugh from her baby boy.

"Act natural," Suzy said hurriedly, whirling around to stand next to him. She threw her arm around his shoulders and pulled him to her side, knowing they looked anything but natural. Justin barely had enough time to thrust his honey bun behind his back before a purple robe and matching slippers came into view. Suzy prepared an excuse about it being the weekend, and sometimes that meant sugary sweets, when any and all responses died on her tongue.

Justin's honey bun hit the floor. Suzy's grip on his shoulder tightened.

A man walked in behind her mother.

There was a gun in his hand.

"I'M SORRY BUT have we met?"

It was a formality, and the only one James

was going to extend to the stranger. The last two days had been filled with surprises. This woman might be another one he didn't want to experience.

"We haven't, I'm afraid, but I thought it was about time we did."

She held out her hand. A pearl ring was on her index finger and matched her necklace and earrings. A gold Rolex hung on her wrist. Whoever she was, she didn't mind flaunting her wealth. James knew for a fact, thanks to his friend Hale, that the high heels she wore cost more than most people made in three paychecks combined. Fashion aside, how she'd gotten past the deputy guarding the entrance was one of several questions that sprang to mind.

"My name is Katrina," she introduced herself, giving his hand a firm shake. "I'm a friend of Hank's."

James didn't have time to hide his surprise.

"Hank," he repeated cautiously.

She nodded. Her smile hadn't faltered since he'd opened the door.

The red flag that had begun to rise at the time of her arrival shot up.

"Well, to be honest, *friend* isn't as accurate a description as I'd like. He's more of a business associate. One I'm having a hard time finding at the moment. I was hoping you could help me."

"I'm sorry, but I don't know a Hank," he lied, deciding to keep his cards close to his chest. "If it's someone who works at one of the businesses I invest in or help run, then you'll have to be more specific." He put on his best grin. "I'm good with numbers, computers and making breakfast, but I'm afraid I'm bad with names and faces."

Katrina's smile didn't even dim a fraction. She adjusted the bag on her shoulder. "Oh, how silly of me." She laughed. It was soft but not sincere. "I suppose you being at his house earlier today might have been misleading. Per-

haps, instead, you were trying to find someone else?"

James held his ground. Every muscle in his
face was working overtime to not give away
what he was thinking.

"I don't know what you're talking about," he
said, deciding he wanted to see her work for
the answer she wanted, hopefully revealing
her hand in the process. How did she know
he'd been at Hank's? Had she been watching
him? Why would she? Did she know for a fact
he was lying? "Aside from a trip to the city to
help close on a deal for work, I've been here
all day," he lied again.

Her smile grew wider. Instead of it adding
more charm, it started to degrade her beauty.
He'd hit a nerve.

"Mr. Callahan. James, if I may. I'm here to
help."

"I don't understand what with. Even if I did
know your Hank, it seems like you're here
because you need *my* help. Not the other way

around." He shrugged. "Which I also don't know how to give."

The briefest of muscle twitches ran along her jaw.

Something was wrong.

Katrina was wrong. His feeling only heightened when she responded.

"I would say I'd offer you compensation for your insight, but I guess it's hard to tempt someone like yourself with something as trivial as money. So, why don't I do this—" She looked down at her watch. James waited, alarm rising in his gut. "If you tell me what you know about Hank and where he is, then I won't order my man in your house to gut your sister."

Katrina raised her head and met his gaze. Her smile was back. It was genuine.

James didn't have time to process what she'd said.

A scream tore through the house.

"Don't worry," Katrina added quickly. "That

was just to prove to you that that man is really *in* the house. I call the shots. And before you go all hero on me, let me make something crystal clear."

She took a step closer, straddling the door frame. One foot in and one foot out of his family's home.

"The only way your sister's insides remain inside is if I tell him not to touch her. You silence me, you kill her."

James's body vibrated with so many emotions, he couldn't sort out even one.

Katrina leaned in, still smiling. "Now, Mr. Callahan, be a good boy and invite me inside. It's been a long day already. I don't have all night."

RAGE AND FEAR coursed through Suzy, nearly blinding her. Luckily it didn't take over completely. She was able to hold on to enough clarity to recognize the man.

"Hank?" The bar owner had changed clothes

and was wearing a hat. It did little to cover the gash across his eyebrow or the bruising around his eye. "What the h—"

"Grayton McKenzie is on his way to grab you," he interrupted. "You need to leave. *Now.*"

"What? How do you know?"

Suzy loosened her grip on Justin. Her mother's eyes were as wide as saucers. If the gun had been aimed at her, Suzy bet they would have fallen out of her face.

"Criminal grapevine," he said in a rush. "I maybe have a five-minute start on him. If you want out, you gotta go." As she had in the bar that morning, Suzy believed Hank's sincerity. Still, when he reached into his pocket, she got a little antsy. He pulled out a piece of paper. "Here's Patricia's private number. She knows to expect your call. She has the boy, but will only give him to you or Callahan. If you don't get him by tomorrow morning, she's leaving town with him and never coming back. You got that?"

Suzy took the paper and nodded. "What about you? You're not coming with us?"

Hank shook his head.

"I'm done being ambushed by that scrawny son of a—" He paused, looked at Justin and chose new words. "I'm tired of looking over my shoulder and seeing Grayton McKenzie. So I'm going to do something about that. To-night. Now hurry!"

Hank moved past them to the front of the house to keep a lookout while Suzy grabbed her mother and son by the hand and ran for the bedroom closet. Opening her gun safe took less than ten seconds, but it felt like hours to her.

"Here, Mom, take this." She handed over her personal handgun.

"Suzy—" Her mother started to object.

"Don't you do that," Suzy interrupted. "You

were married to a cop. You can use a gun if you need to."

Suzy didn't wait for a response but led them through the house, grabbing her cell phone from the chair and the keys from the wall hooks in the entryway, and then all three were converging on the car.

"You drive," Suzy ordered her mother, tossing her the keys. Despite being in a purple bathrobe, scared, confused and wielding a gun she didn't want to be holding, Cordelia Simmons knew when she needed to listen to her daughter. She threw open the driver's-side door while Suzy pulled the back door open and all but pushed Justin in. She handed her phone to him. "You *stay down* and call Billy. Tell him Grayton is coming to the house. Can you do that?"

Justin's eyes were wide, terrified, but he nodded. It broke Suzy's heart, but she didn't have the time to reassure him. While she hadn't said it out loud yet, she'd already made a decision she knew her mother wasn't going to like.

She leaned in and kissed his forehead, then turned to her mom. "Drive straight to the station. Keep a normal speed so as not to bring attention to yourself. Keep Billy on the phone. Don't stop for anyone." Suzy threw the paper Hank had given her into the front seat. "When you get there, make sure James Callahan gets that number."

"You can't stay," her mother said, voice cracking.

"He knows who I am and where I live. This might be our only chance to get him."

Their eyes met, and then her mother glanced at Justin. She didn't say it out loud, but both women understood that it wasn't just their lives that were endangered by Grayton. Justin's was, too.

"You be safe, baby girl."

Suzy nodded. "I plan on it," she said with a quick smile. "Love you both."

The moment she shut the door, the car reversed. Suzy didn't move until it was turning at the end of the street. It was like watching her heart drive away.

She shook her head. Now it was time to focus.

She ran back into the house.

"We're not going to kill him if we can help it," Suzy told Hank, voice firm. "We're going to trap him. That's not a request. That's an order."

Hank didn't argue. "Your house, your rules."

It caught Suzy off guard, but she gave him a nod. "Good."

Hank turned back to the window. His entire body tensed.

Suzy hurried to his side and looked out. On the street where her mother and child had been traveling less than a minute ago was a black SUV.

"Whatever we're about to do, we need to decide on a plan," he said. "Fast."

Chapter Fifteen

"Now, now, James, don't blow a gasket," Katrina started. "She's fine as long as we're fine."

James sat down heavily. Angry didn't cover it. He was furious.

Katrina had pulled her gun from her name-brand purse just after Chelsea had screamed. She marched him back into the kitchen, where he was now at the table, their supper still fresh on their plates. A man with a matching gun and a myriad of rough descriptors that indicated he would hurt James's little sister if ordered to held one of Chelsea's arms. He'd pulled her from the table and had her a few feet away, near the side door that led outside.

James didn't like how easily they could use it to escape with her in tow.

Chelsea's eyes were wide but dry.

"What do you want?" James growled.

Katrina's smile finally took a turn for the tainted. It was chilling.

But nothing compared to the fire of rage he was feeling.

"The same thing I wanted at the door," she said, sliding into the chair opposite him. She leaned over to take a piece of bacon. "I just want information on Hank. For instance, why you were at his place this morning talking to a detective." James gritted his teeth. Katrina held her hand and the bacon up. "Let me preface whatever it is you're about to say with the reminder that I'm the only thing standing in the way of him producing a lot of pain in your baby sister.

"I know, I'm a broken record, but if I'm happy, they're happy. And I'm happy when I'm not being lied to. And I'm *very* good at knowing when I'm being lied to." She took a bite of the bacon. "Speaking of, I now know you weren't lying about being good at cooking breakfast foods," she said around the bite. "So, was that the only truth you told me?"

She wasn't unstable. Of that much James was certain. Instead, she was precise. From her wardrobe to her hair, from the way she walked and carried herself to the way her eyes never left his, she was very much a woman who knew what she wanted. James had no doubt she would do whatever it took to get it, too.

One look at Chelsea, and he decided he'd stick to the truth, or some of it, at least. He wasn't about to gamble with her life. Which also meant not telling the very determined, seemingly devious woman across from him that they were the siblings of the infamous Gardner Todd.

"I was with a Riker County Sheriff's Department deputy when she got a call from a woman about some people breaking into her neighbor's house. I convinced her to let me tag along."

Katrina's perfectly shaped eyebrows rose. "And why would you want to do that?"

"I may be good at business, but that doesn't mean I'm always excited about it. When I heard the call and saw we were close, I thought it would be more fun than crunching numbers all morning." He shrugged. "When we got there no one else was around. More deputies and local PD showed up after, and I tried to get the story of who lived there from the detective on scene. All he said was that a man named Hank was missing."

"Then why did you lie to me on the doorstep?"

"I don't know you." He spelled it out. "I didn't want you thinking I was involved with someone I wasn't on the off chance it got me or my loved ones in trouble." He nodded to Chelsea and the man. "Case in point, the goon holding my baby sister at gunpoint while *you* hold a gun on *me*."

Katrina leaned back in the chair without sacrificing her upright posture.

"So, that's it? You rode with your deputy friend to a potential crime scene and then just casually talked to a detective while there?"

James nodded. It was the truth, more or less. Enough that he could confidently say yes, anyway.

Katrina studied his expression before turning to the men and Chelsea. "And what were you doing today, little one?" she asked.

Chelsea didn't hesitate. "I drove here from school."

Her voice was even. It didn't waver one bit. James couldn't help but be proud. He looked back at Katrina. She seemed thoughtful.

Which, in itself, was troubling.

James's muscles tightened as she pushed back her chair and stood.

"So I guess I barged in here for no reason,

then," she said with a laugh. "How impolite! My apologies, Mr. Callahan."

She surprised James by putting the gun back in her purse. Her lackey, however, didn't lower his from Chelsea's side. "For your hospitality, I'd like to do you a favor now."

She put her bag down on the table and reached into her pocket.

"I had a boy in grade school who was obsessed with me. Followed me around, constantly passed me notes and even once snuck into the girls' bathroom to try to talk to me. He was a mess, I tell you. Always trying to steal a kiss from me or trying to look up my skirt. He tried it all, really, until one day I yelled at him to leave me alone in front of all of his little friends."

She rolled her eyes. "Oh, how it hurt his little pride. To try to save face, and his ego, he turned his obsession into anger. Started calling me names, throwing food at me in the cafeteria and even placing some roadkill in my locker once. I thought, given time, he'd get bored, but he never did."

She sighed, as if recalling a mildly annoying memory. "So, one day, I confronted him again. I told him *very clearly* that if he didn't stop his pathetic attempts at trying to earn the other little boys' respect, I would make him stop. I'll never forget his laugh. He told me, and I quote, 'You're just some little girl. What are you gonna do?'"

Hand still in her pocket, she walked around the table and stopped at his side. She leaned back against the table, eyes never leaving his. "He didn't listen to my warning. Put a stink bomb in my *new* locker. Horrible smell. I swear, still to this day, I catch whiffs of it. Oh, just the worst." She shook her head. The humor that she'd been telling the story with started to disappear.

"So I did what I had promised him," she continued, voice going arctic. "I swiped a kitchen knife from Home Ec, lured him into a supply closet and carved the words *little girl* into his skin."

She finally pulled her hand out of her pocket. It was holding a closed compact knife.

"He never forgot who I was, and you better believe my locker was never home to anything other than my books after that. I can't be all that mad at him, though," she continued with a shrug. "He taught me the lesson I'm about to teach you."

Her smile came back.

James didn't like it one bit.

Especially not when it was followed by her opening the knife. The blade was small but undoubtedly sharp. Definitely a blade that could—and would—do damage, depending on the determination of the person wielding it.

"And what lesson was that?" he asked, trying to show the woman that she didn't scare him. That she didn't have the upper hand.

Even though she did.

On both points.

She looked at the blade for a moment before answering. "Underestimating a woman like me is not only foolish, it's dangerous." She flipped the knife around in her hand so quickly that James knew, without a doubt, he was about to learn how sharp it really was. "You may be telling me some of the truth, but we both know you're holding back on me, James." She held the knife up to his cheek. Chelsea gasped. "And I know why." She ran the knife slowly down his skin, careful not to break it.

"Just like that boy in grade school, you believe that my wrath isn't worthy of your compliance." The knife stopped at his jawline. She moved it off his face altogether. "However, unlike that boy from grade school, you're a man. One who has served in the military, become a business tycoon and even become a savior in your own right. I'm smart enough to know that simply carving my name into you won't get me what I want."

She moved off the table and over to the man. With a single nod from her, he changed positions. He stepped away from Chelsea and adjusted the end of his gun so it was aimed toward James.

James's heart hammered in his chest. He stood slowly.

It didn't stop Katrina from moving to stand behind his sister. She grabbed the hem of Chelsea's T-shirt and pulled it up and off her body, throwing it to the bottom of the stairs.

James balled his fists, already knowing what was coming.

"But I think it's a safe bet that carving my name into *her* skin might get that pretty mouth of yours moving." Katrina pressed the knife to Chelsea's chest, stopping above her sports bra and right next to the chain of her necklace.

The same gold heart necklace Chelsea had worn almost every day since she was ten. The same one James had given her the day he'd officially become her guardian.

The same one he'd clasped around her neck while promising her that he'd always, *always* protect her.

"Stop."

Katrina pulled the knife up, hovering above Chelsea's skin. She raised her eyebrows again.

"Ready to tell me what you're trying to hide already?" She gave him a dramatic pout. "Are you sure you don't want me to at least *try* to convince you? I've nearly perfected my knife—"

"I went looking for Hank to try to get information on Gardner Todd," he interrupted. There was no point leaving his brother's name out of it. He might not know Katrina, but he did know that she wouldn't let that detail be ignored.

Her eyebrows went as high as they could. She was genuinely surprised.

"And why would a man like James Callahan be looking for information on a man like

Gardner Todd? A dead man at that, I might add."

He didn't hesitate. Not even for a second.

"Because he was my brother," he said. He nodded toward Chelsea. "He was *our* brother."

No one spoke for what felt like a long time. James didn't move his gaze from Katrina's, afraid that looking away might create suspicion at what he'd just said.

The red-haired woman seemed to be frozen, eyebrows high and knife low. Her goon wasn't as guarded with his expressions. There weren't many criminals in the South—and James was positive that was exactly what Katrina and her goon were—who didn't know Gardner's name. The news that he had a brother and that brother was a Callahan...well, that surprise showed clearly across the goon's face.

So much so that he didn't seem to notice movement behind him on the stairs. Katrina and Chelsea didn't, either.

Though James already knew who it must be.

"Gardner had no living family," Katrina finally said. "I even had some of my best look into it. You're lying."

Katrina pressed the knife back to Chelsea's skin. His sister whimpered.

"Let her go and I'll prove it to you," James said hurriedly.

"How?" This time she didn't pull the knife back.

"Upstairs, in my office," he started. "I have boxes and boxes of family pictures. There are even some on top of my desk already. I pulled them out this morning before I went to Hank's. Go take a look for yourself." There was movement on the stairs again, but James only had eyes for Katrina and her knife.

"So, the *savior* of Bates Hill kept Gardner Todd a secret."

"I did," he admitted again. He took two steps forward. The man with the gun glanced at Katrina. She didn't address his concern. "You got

what you want. Let her go. You know everything I do now."

"You can't just drop a bomb like that and not
have a shock wave follow it," she was quick to
say. "I can't believe that's all you know."

Up until that moment, Katrina had only become overtly serious when talking about the
lesson she wanted to teach James. Everything
else had been peppered with smiles and dark
humor. Yet something shifted now. Her eyes
narrowed. Her lips straightened.

She tightened the grip on the knife, but
pulled it away from Chelsea.

"James, what other secrets do you know?"
With one decisive step forward, she came
within striking distance. "And if you're *really* Gardner's brother, how come you don't
know about me? Or is your acting better than
I thought?"

James wanted to know the answer to that,
too. Who was Katrina? What was her connection to Gardner? To Hank?

That was when it clicked.

James felt so stupid not to have put it together until then. Still, he needed her to say it.

"Why do you need to find Hank?"

Katrina's eyes burned bright and angry. No humor. No charm. No performance for the sake of performance. She lowered her voice. It was as sharp as her blade. "Because Gardner gave him something of mine, and I fully intend to get it back."

James didn't move a muscle. She was so close he could smell her perfume.

"What did he take?"

James held his breath.

Katrina looked murderous.

"He took my son."

Chapter Sixteen

James wished a lot of things.

He wished he'd talked to his brother more. He wished he'd made more of an effort to get him out of his life of crime. He wished he could go out on the back patio and have a beer with his older brother and talk about something as normal as football.

He wished he knew why his brother had kept his son a secret, what he'd planned to do with him and how James had fit into that plan.

Standing opposite Katrina, seeing Chelsea over her shoulder without a shirt on, terrified, he knew exactly why Gardner had tried to keep his son away from the woman.

His brother might have been considered bad, but James had a feeling Katrina was nothing but evil.

"Your lack of surprise is telling, Mr. Callahan," Katrina bit out. "Where. Is. My. Son?"

She brought the knife up to his throat.

It was the wrong move.

"Now!" James yelled.

Chaos exploded in the kitchen.

James grabbed Katrina's wrist just as Queso jumped out from the stairwell, wielding a bat. He slammed it down across the goon's back. The man stumbled forward. His gun clattered to the ground near James's feet. Katrina brought her foot up and tried to kick James between the legs, but he was faster. He blocked the kick with his free hand and then pushed the woman as far from him as he could.

Katrina's man wasn't down for the count, however. He regained his footing and roared, turning to face Queso. The boy had repositioned himself between Chelsea and the raging bull.

James dived for the gun. He needed to stop the fighting. If Katrina and her guy got the upper hand again, James and Chelsea would pay for it with their lives.

Yet Katrina was fast, too. She came screaming at him with her knife brandished high. With another war cry, she brought the blade down. He kept quiet as the blade slid against the skin on his back; he was focused on one thing.

"Stop!" he yelled, gripping the gun and rolling to avoid Katrina's knife again. He jumped up and trained the gun on her. The henchman didn't care. He took a swing at Queso. Chelsea screamed as the boy took the hit across the face.

But he wasn't about to go down that easily.

Queso executed what James would later look back on as the perfect swing. The bat connected with the man's gut. It stopped him in his tracks. This time when he staggered, he fell. Hard.

He didn't move—but his boss did.

"Stop," James repeated, taking a more disciplined stance. She was crouched down, coiling like a snake ready to pounce. He needed to make sure she didn't. "I'm not above shooting you," he added. "Drop the knife."

Katrina's eyes narrowed. They flitted between James and the gun, Queso and the bat, and then back to the gun. She decided to relent. The knife clattered to the kitchen floor.

"Chelsea, you okay?" James asked. In his peripheral vision, he saw her nod.

"Y-yeah. I'm good now."

"Go upstairs and call the sheriff's department from my office. Lock the door behind you."

Her voice was small but steady. "Okay."

He waited until he heard retreating footsteps to look at Queso. Blood gushed down his chin from a busted lip. Still, he grinned. "I told you bad *guys* don't ring doorbells."

Katrina didn't speak as they waited for the authorities. She didn't even object as James bound her to one of the dining room chairs using bungee cords from the garage that he sent Queso after. Her friend said even less as the two of them hog-tied the man.

"One hell of a punch you took there," James said while inspecting the makeshift knots behind the man's arms and legs. "Even better swing you gave back with that bat." James lowered his voice so Katrina couldn't hear. "Thank you for helping us out."

The boy pushed his hands into his pockets. He shrugged, trying for nonchalance.

"Thanks for being a rich dude with two sets of stairs. I wouldn't have been able to get the drop on big guy here without them."

When things calmed down, he'd make sure Queso knew how much James appreciated what he'd done, risking his life to save them.

Until then, the best he could do was clap the boy on the shoulder, smile and go back to the task at hand.

He walked past Katrina to his cell phone, which was face down on the table. He had sent Chelsea upstairs to use the landline to put distance between her and Katrina, but now it was time to make his own calls.

Though someone had already called him. A missed-call notification scrolled across the middle of the screen. James didn't recognize the number. The voice-mail icon was next to it. He moved away so Katrina couldn't hear and played the message.

It was the sheriff. "This is Billy. Something happened at Suzy's house. Call me. ASAP."

James's stomach went cold.

When he looked at Katrina, all she did was smile.

SUZY ROLLED BACK her shoulder. It hurt. The pain must have shown on her face.

"You sure you don't want to go to the hospital?" Billy asked, cowboy hat in his hand. The day had been so long that he hadn't had the chance to hang it up when it turned night. Now he looked like a tired Alabama cowboy, leaning against the front wall of the sheriff's department, bathed in the glow of the streetlight not too far from the front steps. Suzy wondered how she looked next to him.

The last hour had been nothing short of tiring.

After her mom drove off, Justin had followed through with the plan. He'd called Billy, and soon the sheriff and his deputies were speeding toward the house. Billy had gotten there in time to watch Suzy tackle Grayton's backup, a man twice her size. The move had been her way of saying thank-you to Hank for the heads-up about Grayton, considering the angry stranger was two seconds away from putting several bullets into the bar owner. After she'd gotten the man to the ground, she'd kept the upper hand while her colleagues and friends helped cuff him.

Hank, however, had never had anything but the upper hand with Grayton. While she may have been angry at him, Hank was riding several waves of fury.

"You tried to get to my Patricia," he'd roared, holding a bleeding Grayton by the scruff of his shirt. "How did you know where to find me? Who do you work for?"

Suzy wanted the same answers, but not at the expense of Hank killing the man. She'd quietly, yet firmly, talked the bar owner away from Grayton while the deputies did their thing.

"None of this makes sense," Hank had said, shaking his head and trying to calm down. He'd jumped Grayton as soon as the man had broken through the back door. There was blood across his face, but Suzy had no idea who it belonged to. "Why does he want the kid?"

An hour later, Suzy was still waiting for that

answer and, more urgently, one Alabama millionaire.

She and Billy had just gotten to the department when Chelsea called in. Matt had been close and had reported that both Callahans and Queso were okay. He was handling the transfer of the woman and man, two people whose identities Suzy didn't yet know.

Two more puzzle pieces.

She just hoped that when James showed up, they could finally finish it.

"I know it's none of my business, but I have to say it," Billy said after a period of silence. His voice was all business. She stiffened, waiting for some kind of admonishment from her boss.

"I think your dad would have really liked James."

That caught Suzy off guard. But she just smiled.

It didn't matter how she felt about James or how he felt about her, because either way, she believed Billy was right. Her father would have absolutely liked the man.

"Thanks, Billy." She meant it.

He shrugged. "I just call it how I see it."

Suzy laughed but cut the rest of the conversation short. The sound of car doors shutting pulled Billy and Suzy along the sidewalk and into the side parking lot. Two deputy cruisers drove to the back. Matt's Tahoe broke away from the line and slid into his parking spot. Suzy's stomach tightened. While she knew that James was okay, seeing was believing.

Four doors opened. Matt and Queso stepped out of one side. Chelsea walked around the back soon after. Then came James. Jeans had never looked so good on a man.

Suzy held her ground as he found her gaze.

Matt was the first to talk. "We have a situation," he began. "One I think should stay private until we get a better handle on it."

"Let's go talk in the conference room," Billy

offered. He glanced at Suzy. "I think it's time we got on the same page."

He led Matt back to the front of the building. Queso nodded to Suzy but kept at Chelsea's side as they followed. James lagged behind. He was frowning.

"Are you okay?" he asked. "Matt told me what happened."

Something was off in his tone. It sounded hard—cold, even. Detached.

Still she nodded. "Yeah, nothing some Icy Hot and Advil can't take care of. You?"

He didn't nod. "I'll be better when this is all done."

He followed the group without another word. Like she was a stranger. Suzy couldn't deny it hurt a little, even though she more than understood it. A lot had happened to the two of them in the last few days.

But that night?

That night was different.

Grayton had come to Suzy's home. If Hank

hadn't been there, who knew what would have happened to Justin? To her mother. A town over, James hadn't had a warning. By the looks on all three of their faces, she knew something bad had happened before their intruders had been detained.

They marched through the lobby and the hall to the conference room. Billy stepped to the side, next to the door, and motioned for Matt, Queso and Chelsea to go in. Suzy reached out and caught James's hand before he could follow. She nodded to Billy, and the sheriff went inside the room without them.

"What?" James asked, frown still firmly in place. The contact of her hand evidently did nothing to improve his mood, but he didn't pull away, either.

"Hank showed up and warned me about Grayton being on his way. He gave me and my mother and Justin time to escape, but I didn't want him to get away again, so I decided to stay," she said. "But *before* I made that decision, he gave me a number to call Patricia." James's eyes widened but she hurried on. "Hank said if either you or I didn't call that number by the morning, he'd told Patricia to take the baby and leave town."

"We need to call it," James said before she could get another word out. "I filled Matt in about what happened during the ride over. He can tell Billy what happened. We need to call Patricia and—"

Suzy smiled. It clearly deflated his urgency enough to stop his current train of thought.

"You already called?"

She nodded. "I did."

Wrapping her fingers fully around his hand, Suzy pulled him to the office opposite the sheriff's. The nameplate read Chief Deputy Simmons, and it always made her feel a rush of pride.

Suzy opened the door wide. Justin looked around from behind the computer screen and smiled. Opposite him, in an oversize chair that

Suzy had brought in herself, was her mother. In her arms was a baby boy.

"Patricia told me where she was and said I should meet her and get him," she said. "So I did that, too."

Chapter Seventeen

James's entire expression changed. Like God himself had reached through the roof and grabbed the burden of guilt and worry straight from his shoulders.

"That's him," James said, sounding almost unsure. But his steps were less uncertain. Suzy's mother stood so he could get a better view. "That's *him*." He peered down at the baby, seeing his green eyes, mop of golden hair and chubby little legs.

"Yep, that's him," Suzy agreed.

James shook his head and laughed. He took the boy in his arms without hesitation.

"No," he said. "I mean his face. It's all Gardner." James let out another loud laugh and stroked the baby's hair. The boy looked alarmed but didn't cry. "And *this hair*! He's got a full head of it! Wow. Suzy, is this a beautiful kid or what?"

James looked at her with such blatant love across his face that she knew right then and there she wanted some for herself.

She wanted some of James.

"He certainly is."

James put his finger against the boy's palm. When he squeezed it, James smiled ear to ear.

"Hey, Justin, why don't we go grab something out of the vending machine in the break room?" Suzy's mom asked, smiling too. "I think your mama and Mr. Callahan need to talk a little bit."

Justin nodded and came around the desk. He stopped next to James, who adjusted the baby so he could see him better.

"I like him, too," Justin said, sure in his words. "I didn't like the crying as much."

All the adults laughed.

"There's a family doctor we all know who's agreed to come in tonight," Suzy said after the door shut behind her mom. "Just to give him a once-over to make sure he's okay." She walked to James's side and played with the boy's little toes. "Patricia confirmed your theory about what happened earlier. She saw two SUVs and only had enough time to run to the neighbors. She met up with Hank after he left the bar. She said with the day they've had, the boy hasn't been able to really sleep, so I imagine he's going to crash hard soon."

"The boy... Did she not know his name?"

Suzy shook her head. She trailed her fingers up to the boy's tummy. He was wearing a onesie with a shark across the middle. She tickled its fin.

"No. According to Hank, Gardner said there was a letter that he wanted to keep with his son at all times just in case something happened to him. It had all of his information, including a birth certificate. Though everything was kept hidden. Hank didn't even know about this adorable little boy until the day Gardner went to meet with you." She looked into the face of a child who would never know his real father and sobered. "Hank looked everywhere but couldn't find it. He said there might be one more place, but it might take a few days to get to."

"Where *is* Hank?"

"Since he's been helping us, not to mention keeping this little guy safe, he and Billy came to an understanding. We won't put him on any official documents as long as he stays somewhere we can reach him at any time. As of right now, he and Patricia have left Riker County." Suzy lowered her voice. "To be honest, I think he ruffled quite a few feathers trying to get information on Grayton and his gang of men."

James stiffened. "I don't think it was Grayton's gang." He sighed and looked down at his nephew. "I think Billy's right. It's time for us all to get on the same page."

GETTING EVERYONE ON the same page was a lot easier with everyone in the same room. Baby Gardner, as they'd decided to call him for the time being, went back into the care of Cordelia and Justin while the rest of their makeshift crew got down to brass tacks.

They went into the conference room with the fragments of the overall picture—from what had happened at Suzy's house with Grayton to everything that Katrina had said at the estate—and were able to form something that finally made sense.

"Katrina and Gardner have a child together, Gardner decides he doesn't want her around the kid, takes Baby Gardner and hides him away with Hank," Detective Walker summarized. "She gets wind somehow that Hank has him and sends Grayton and company to try to find him. In the process, she unwittingly pays a visit to Gardner's brother and sister."

"Where she shows us how insane she really is," Chelsea added. "And apparently how much she likes knives."

She sat with Queso at the end of the table. Meeting her nephew had shaken her out of her fear over what had happened earlier. Though, James was sure, she'd have nightmares about Katrina for some time. Hell, he probably would, too.

"What's going to happen to her now?" James asked. "Last I saw, she definitely wasn't talking."

"Grayton either," Suzy added.

The sheriff cracked a grin. "In my experience, men like Grayton McKenzie are only good at one thing. And that's self-preservation. I think if we apply just the right amount of pressure in just the right place, we can get him to roll over on Katrina. Who, at this point, I'm going to assume is the brains. From what you've told me of her, she doesn't seem to be the follower type."

James had to agree with that.

"Either way, let us worry about the two of them," he continued. "No offense, but all of you look mighty worn out. I think you could do with a good night's sleep. Even if it is technically morning."

The sheriff's gaze went straight to Suzy, who was in the process of opening her mouth. He held up his hand to stop her.

"I'm not about to debate with you on this, Suzy."

"And for once I wasn't about to debate it, either," she responded with a snort. "But my house…"

She let her sentence trail off. Billy swiveled to James.

"I'm sure Mr. Callahan here wouldn't mind helping," he said. "Last I checked, he had more than enough room."

James felt his eyebrows rise. Billy elaborated before Suzy could.

"Before our star quarterback here tackled Grayton, his buddies had a little too much fun with their ammo. Shot up the place really good." Billy paused. "Let me guess," he said. "She didn't tell you *that* part?"

James shook his head. "No, she left that out."

"It's not that bad," she tried. "Just need to call some repairmen out tomorrow to work their magic."

"Not that bad?" Billy repeated. "Suzy, your house looks like Swiss cheese."

Suzy sighed. When she looked back at him, emotions he couldn't read flashed across her face. Then one he knew finally settled. Embarrassment.

"If it's too much, I can book a hotel room, no problem," she said.

James was about to tell her he was more than okay with her staying—in fact, the idea excited him in a different way—when Queso finally spoke up.

"The dude lives in a mansion," he said. "I think he can squeeze in a few more people."

James couldn't help but laugh. "That I can, and I'm more than happy to."

Suzy didn't join in the mirth, but she nodded.

"So, does that mean Baby Gardner gets to come home with us, too?" This time, it was Chelsea who spoke.

The question turned James's mood dark. There was no way, after everything that had happened, that he was leaving his nephew behind.

Luckily he didn't have to say that out loud.

Billy nodded. "Due to the unique nature of this case, for now I'm going to put Baby Gardner into your custody, James," he said. "But first thing Monday morning we're going to have to start the process of legally getting this all sorted and squared away. I assume you're going to want to adopt him?"

It was a question that Chelsea had already asked and he'd already answered, but James realized then that he'd never told the rest of them his plans. Not even Suzy. What did she think of that? Was it too much to handle if something were to happen between them? Having to raise one sibling and then raise a nephew? And a baby to boot? Was that more than the single mom was willing to take on, going from a two-family situation to dating a man who brought two more people into the picture?

Did she even want to take on anything with James in the first place?

And what did he want?

No matter the answer, it wouldn't make a difference. James was proud of his sister and knew he'd be proud of his nephew, too. He'd do his best to provide a loving and stable home for both for as long as he lived.

His family might not have been conventional, but they were his.

"Yes," he answered, unable to hide the pride in his voice. "I do."

Billy smiled. "Then come Monday, we'll see how to go about doing that. Deal?"

James nodded. "That's a deal, Sheriff."

GETTING EVERYONE BACK to the Callahan estate was an adventure. One that included a caravan of Riker County Sheriff's Department vehicles with Suzy's car in the rear. If it was overwhelming for James, he didn't show it. In fact, Suzy got the impression that he liked it.

Even when Baby Gardner started crying as soon as the group got into the entryway of his house.

"This is chaos," Queso said, giving the baby the stink eye.

"But it's the best kind," James responded, holding the car seat in one hand and the diaper bag Patricia had been using in the other.

"Is good chaos even a thing?" Queso asked back, raising his voice over Baby Gardner's cries.

James laughed. Chelsea rolled her eyes.

"If you can take on a man twice your size, I think you can handle being around a crying baby," she said.

Queso scrunched up his nose. "As long as I don't have to change it."

No sooner did the words leave his mouth than the smell of a soiled diaper filled the room.

"Ew, *gross*," Justin said from her side. Suzy mussed his hair.

"Hey, you used to do much worse than that," she teased. Her mother nodded.

"Amen to that," the older woman said.

"Looks like I'm about to change my first baby," James said with a laugh. He motioned to the stairs. "Chelsea, could you show Suzy, Ms. Cordelia and Justin to the guest suite?" He looked at Suzy. "There should be some new clothes and things for you three in there. If you need anything else, let me know."

Suzy's eyebrow rose. "Does that mean Douglas is around?"

James laughed. She liked how much he was doing that, now that they'd found his nephew.

"Yes, he did some shopping for me while we were at the department," he answered. Then he looked to Chelsea, though he spoke to the group as a whole. "There's already been several sweeps over the house to make sure everything is safe. The guards are back and here to stay for a while, just to ease our minds." Then James looked directly at Queso. "The door that was broken into was repaired, and the alarm will be set momentarily. If you have the urge to leave the house to smoke, the entire estate will know it."

"The lesson being, don't smoke," Chelsea muttered.

Queso rolled his eyes this time. "Chief deputy here already crunched my last one," he whined.

Suzy smiled. "And I'd do it again."

"Amen to that," her mother repeated.

It earned a laugh from Chelsea before she started a tour for the only two people who hadn't been in the house yet. Suzy hung back. She wanted to talk to James. But about what, she didn't know. Maybe about the baby. Maybe about Katrina.

Maybe about them.

"Queso, I need to talk to you before you go up," James said, stopping the boy midstep. His expression hardened. He didn't look Suzy's way.

Their one on one would have to wait.

Chapter Eighteen

Douglas had done it again.

He'd managed to pick out sleeping clothes with ease for the new estate guests. Suzy's mother was finally out of her robe and into a matching pajama set that was also purple, while Justin was sporting a Spider-Man shirt and shorts. Suzy was back to sweats and a T-shirt. This time, there was even slippers.

The same slippers she stepped into after an hour of being unable to sleep.

The bed made no complaint as she eased out of it, careful not to jostle her son or mother. While there was another bed they could have used, all three had wound up together. Neither her mom nor Justin wanted to admit it, but they were shaken by what had happened. After Suzy had gotten to the department with Baby Gardner, both had clung to her, trying not to cry.

Suzy traced her sleeping boy's face, peaceful now.

She could admit that the last two days—the last four months, really—had definitely shaken her.

Moonlight streamed through the part in the curtains, helping Suzy navigate the unfamiliar room to the door. She held her breath as it clicked open. A small light in the hallway showed a quiet second floor. Queso's and Chelsea's doors were shut. James's office door was not. A faint light pooled on the hardwood.

Like a moth to a flame, Suzy was drawn to it.

And like he'd been expecting her, James was already smiling.

"Glad to see I'm not the only one who can't

sleep," he greeted her, voice low. He stood next to his desk, the box of pictures in his hand.

"I think we're definitely in the minority on that front."

A baby monitor with a camera attached sat on the side table next to the couch that was opposite the desk. Definitely a new addition since yesterday—they were closing in on four in the morning. Suzy moved around to the front of the monitor and took in the view. The image of a sleeping baby made her heart warm. Being a single mother had been hard, especially when Justin had been that size, but Suzy couldn't help but miss it sometimes. The baby phase didn't stick around, even if their mother's love for them did.

"I just got him down," James said at her shoulder. "I came in here so I wouldn't wake him back up since I couldn't pass out as fast as he did. He's had one heck of a day."

"One thing I think every parent envies is their kids' ability to fall asleep at the drop of a hat." She sighed. She wasn't frustrated or angry. It was just an observation. One of many she realized she wanted to share with the man.

Suzy turned and was surprised at how close he was. A warmth of a different nature started to spread within her. Especially when she realized that the last time they'd been in the room they'd been in a lip-lock.

Twice.

"So, let me guess," Suzy started, putting some mental distance between his body and hers. "Douglas did more than shop for clothes while we were at the sheriff's department?"

James chuckled. "Big-time," he confirmed. "If he wasn't a friend, I think he would have up and quit. Thankfully, he took pity on me. He even bought a crib. Which I coaxed Queso into helping me put together." He smirked. "The kid's pretty good with his hands. Fast, too. Whines a little too much, but I think he's frustrated."

His smile dropped. A sigh pushed out and

followed him as he moved around to the back of his desk. He pushed the chair aside, opened the top drawer and waved her over.

"I didn't say anything earlier because the whole Katrina thing really threw me, and then we saw Baby Gardner—which by the way, I really hope Hank pulls through with his birth certificate so we can stop calling him that—and it went out of my mind but…"

Suzy came to his side and accepted a card he pulled out. It was smaller than a normal business card and completely black. She ran her finger over the top of it. There was an indentation.

"It's in the shape of a butcher's knife," James explained.

"One of Sully's calling cards?" she guessed.

He shook his head. "That's Sully's card, period." He leaned against the desk facing the office's one window. Through the gap in the curtains, Suzy could see the dark trees in the distance. It was comforting in a way. Foreboding in another. "I spent a lot of time and money trying to find someone, *anyone*, who could get me information on Gardner. After months of rumors and hearsay, one name stuck out. The Butcher. It wasn't until I got the name Sully that I was able to set up a meeting. I'm assuming that, because of my status in the public eye, he met with me without his normal cloak-and-dagger routine. Which is good, because it's what he's known for." James tapped the card. "For instance, one of his unique practices is this. It's his ID, essentially. One that encompasses who he is. One he'd never let go."

"Where did you get it?"

James managed to look sheepish. "Out of Katrina's purse."

Suzy opened her mouth to point out this was the type of information to share in an official capacity and not behind closed doors in their pajamas. But James held up his hand to stop the thought before it could spring out.

"I know, I know. I shouldn't have taken it, but once I did I got sidetracked with everything else and forgot about it." He gave her a small smile. "I was going to tell you in the morning. Well, *later* in the morning."

Suzy ran her fingers over the engraved knife again.

"You think Katrina killed Sully." It wasn't a question.

James's frown was back. It deepened. Suzy put the card in the drawer and shut it. She was sure she knew him well enough to pick up on his unspoken thoughts.

"You can't be everyone's father," she reminded him.

"No, I can't," he agreed. "But I can be a friend."

It was such a pure sentiment that Suzy couldn't help but reach out. She cupped his face and with a genuine smile told him the truth.

"You're a good man, James Callahan," she said. "Don't let anyone ever tell you any differently."

It was one of the observations she had wanted to share with him. She had done it because she believed it needed to be said, not because she'd hoped for anything in return. So when he caught her hand as she pulled it away, Suzy didn't know how to react. Not right away.

Instead, she gave him a questioning look.

He returned the look. However, there seemed to be no question in his.

Slowly, as if he was trying not to spook her, he pulled her hand up to his mouth and turned so her palm was open toward him. Even more slowly, he brushed his lips against the skin of her palm. It took the breath right out of her.

Confusion melted away, replaced by something hotter.

His eyes found hers as he wrapped his other hand around her hip. Suzy felt her eyes widen. James's crystal blues held her gaze. He stood, and just as slowly as he'd done with her palm, he pulled her body to his. He kept her stare, as if waiting for her to deny him. Or simply waiting for her to stop him.

She would do neither.

His body was warm against hers, even through their clothes. Suzy's breathing had gone shallow. She searched his expression for proof that he was as affected by her as she was by him.

She found it in a kiss.

A warm and soft beginning turned to something hard and needy. And this time James didn't seem to have any plans to end it. One of his hands slid into her hair, while the other continued to rest on her hip. Keeping her close. Keeping her against him. Not that Suzy intended to pull away.

She maneuvered under his shirt, desperate to feel his skin against hers. He broke the kiss long enough to show he wanted the same thing. Soon both of their shirts were at their feet, and Suzy was staring down at a chest that shouldn't be real.

In fact, she laughed.

James didn't waste time and covered her mouth with his. It was a softer kiss. "Shh, woman," he whispered, pulling back a little but still keeping close. "If you wake the baby then I'm sending you in there. Why are you laughing, anyway?"

Suzy placed her palm against his stomach and grinned. "Not only are you a charming millionaire but you have abs of steel, too. It just doesn't seem fair for the rest of us simple folks."

James's smile disappeared. So did Suzy's. Had she offended him?

Before she could ask the dark-haired, sexy-as-hell millionaire, he did something else to surprise her. In one fluid movement, he picked her up and carried her to the love seat, only stopping long enough to lock the door.

Suzy tensed, waiting for the drop, but James was gentle. He eased her against the cushions, the cool of the leather sending a chill over her exposed skin. It wasn't until he was on top of her that she really got a show.

Starting at her neck, James trailed his lips down to her collarbone. She curled up against him when he got to her breasts. He thumbed her nipple until it puckered. His mouth and tongue took over next, eliciting raw pleasure in her. It was all she could do not to moan as he treated the other one to the same play.

When he was satisfied he'd been fair to the second nipple, he moved down to her waistband, where his kisses turned hard. Everything in Suzy was on fire, and somehow still managing to get hotter. James hooked the inside of her pants and, for the first time in her life, she praised God that she wasn't wearing her tight jeans. He slid them down and off in a second flat.

Then he did Suzy's work for her, which was good. She was already having a hard time not attacking the man. She didn't just want to be with him. She needed it. She needed him.

He threw his pants on the floor next to hers and lowered himself on top of her slowly, pressing against her and showing Suzy exactly how excited he was by her. Suzy couldn't help the small moan that escaped.

James seemed to enjoy it, but before he could show her how much, he looked into her eyes and smiled.

"Suzanne Simmons, you are anything but simple."

JAMES WOKE UP when he hit the floor. Pain spread through his side and across the cut he'd bandaged at the department. For a second he didn't understand why either hurt and, even more confusing, why he was on the floor. Then the details started to filter in.

First the floor—a burgundy rug on hardwood—then the couch he was staring ahead at—dark leather, a bit worn—and the last clue that reminded him where he was—the blanket that was half on the couch and half covering him up.

He was in his office.

Naked.

And he'd fallen off of the couch because it was definitely smaller than the bed he was used to.

The door was shut, but the room was bright. Sunlight was leaking around the curtains, meaning there was a good chance the rest of the house was awake. It was a thought that sent him scrambling. He jumped up, tripped over the blanket caught between his legs and barely missed falling flat against the floor. Again.

It wasn't until he found his footing that he even thought to look for Suzy.

The last time he'd seen her she'd been on the couch with him, wrapped in his arms and also very naked.

Now?

Now all he could find was his clothes.

He hurriedly put them on, trying to get his

bearings—where was Suzy? What time was it? Did anyone know he was asleep in the office and naked to boot?—when he spotted his phone on the desktop.

He cursed beneath his breath. It was nearly eleven.

"Why didn't you wake me, Suzy?" he mumbled to himself while unlocking his phone. He had a new text message but nothing else.

It so happened the lone message was from the chief deputy herself.

You needed the rest. Don't worry, I'll take care of Baby G.

James let out a breath and smiled. He realized that trusting Suzy had always come easy.

The next few minutes were spent rushing through a shower that he had to admit felt great. Maybe, like she'd said, he really *had* needed some rest. He couldn't remember the last time he'd slept so soundly. Finally having Gardner's son had been a big part of that, he was sure. Just as James was sure having Suzy with him had helped, too.

When she'd told him he was a good man, it was like a piece of him that had always been missing fell into place.

And making love to her?

That was another feeling he wanted to experience again. Preferably many more times.

By the time he was dressed, he could have almost laughed at how excited he was to see her again. Like he was a schoolboy nursing the mother of all crushes.

He even skipped the last two steps on the stairs before sliding into the kitchen with more pep than he'd had in years.

Nothing was going to ruin his good mood, he decided.

So he was nowhere near prepared for the sight that greeted him.

Douglas was laid out on the top of the kitchen island. Blood pooled around him, dripping off the counter and onto the floor. James's own blood turned to ice.

Grayton McKenzie stood from his chair at the table, a gun already aimed at James.

The man smiled.

"You have only two options. You come with me, or they die," the man said. He shrugged. "It's as simple as that."

Chapter Nineteen

Suzy was going to be sick. Her head throbbed; her body throbbed; everything in the room throbbed. Light was pain. Sound was pain. *Breathing* was pain. If it wasn't guaranteed to hurt, she would have yelled out.

Not that she thought it would do any good.

The raw pain at her wrists, along with the full-body ache brought on by gravity, spelled out a situation that turned her stomach even more.

She was hanging up by her wrists, shackled to chains that were connected to metal beams in the ceiling. A ceiling that wasn't a normal ceiling. Suzy fought to find her footing against the concrete floor. The moment she was able to stand up, the pain in her arms and hands lessened considerably.

But that was the only good news for her.

Not only had she been jumped in James's house, she'd been brought back to the one place she'd never thought she'd visit again.

"It's a bit dramatic, I know."

Suzy whipped her head around so fast she whimpered at the pain. Katrina walked into view. There was blood across her white pant-suit. She motioned to the room around them. "But bringing you back to where this all started? Well, I thought it was worth being a *tad* dramatic."

Suzy couldn't help but look at the spot in the corner of the large room.

It was where she'd found Gardner, murdered, four months ago.

"Where's the boy?" Suzy asked, fighting through the fear beginning to spread within her.

Katrina raised an eyebrow.

"Which one?" she asked, feigning confusion. "My boy, your boy or *that* poor excuse of a boy?" Her dark eyes slid behind Suzy. She turned, igniting more pain, and saw someone else hanging in the warehouse.

Queso's body was completely slack. His face was covered in blood and bruises.

"Don't worry—he's alive," Katrina assured her when Suzy turned back to face her. "I'm smart enough to know that if I killed either one of you, James would feel personally responsible for your deaths. When I negotiate with him, I need him to be relatively calm. Which I don't think he'd be if I had let Grayton continue to beat on that one there." She took a few steps closer. The *click* of her heels echoed around them. "Plus, since *your* boy wasn't at the estate, I had to improvise. I knew you'd cooperate if I had someone to hold over you."

"Then why did you knock me unconscious?" Suzy ground out.

Katrina smirked. "Because I know you now, Suzanne Simmons. You would have looked for an opening and taken it to try to stop me. You might have even succeeded since I'm low on men at the moment." She laughed. "Though I have to admit that it did feel good. Maybe it's better that your son didn't see you go down so easily."

Suzy's muscles tensed. She didn't want to give anything away about Justin. Especially if Katrina was thinking of trying to get him as some kind of leverage. Less than a half hour before Grayton and Katrina had shown up, Chelsea had taken Justin and Suzy's mother to the mall in Kipsy. She had a list of things to get the baby, and Suzy suggested they make a day of it. Justin had perked right up. So had her mother. They needed the distraction, the fun. It had only been Suzy, the baby and Queso in the kitchen when Katrina and her men had come in, guns blazing.

"As for *my* son, well, that's none of your

business," Katrina continued. "Gardner should never have taken him in the first place." Her words turned bitter. She crossed her arms over her chest. Suzy had so many questions for her. How had she gotten out of the sheriff's department, for starters? Yet she became transfixed by the woman. If happiness was contagious, hatred was consuming.

"The damn fool thought he could pull one over on me," Katrina continued. "Thought he could slip quietly out into the night with *my* flesh and blood and I not know?" She laughed. It was more of a cackle. One that was born of frustration and anger, long built up, if Suzy had to guess.

"Killing him was too easy a punishment, if you ask me."

A surge of anger went through Suzy. While she hadn't specifically talked to James about who had hired Lester to kill him, once Katrina had shown herself, it seemed obvious. It was one of the questions Matt had been hoping to ask before they'd left the department for the estate.

Now Suzy at least had confirmation of that theory.

"But that man was nothing if not quick on his feet when needed. Well connected, too," Katrina added. "I guess if he *hadn't* had a few tricks up his sleeve, he wouldn't have been the infamous Alabama Boogeyman. Not that that did him any good in the end."

"What do you want with James?" Suzy asked. While she wanted to know everything that had led Gardner to the warehouse months ago, Suzy had to be more concerned with the future. Especially since the present involved her and Queso chained while a no-doubt vicious woman ranted and raved, flipping between pure anger that Suzy could almost feel and malicious pride at what she'd done. There was no telling how she would react to James, considering he'd already bested her once.

She didn't seem the type of person who took kindly to losing.

The smirk she adopted could mean a number of things. She took a step closer and lowered her voice. "For all his hype and glory, Gardner believed in moderation. That included money. Money he never seemed to warm up to telling me the location of, or even how much he had. Instead of spending any more of *my* money and time looking for it, I'm going to go to another, more viable source."

"James," Suzy offered.

Katrina nodded. "The golden-boy savior himself." She snorted. "Heck, if I had known the connection, I would have had Gardner killed a lot sooner and tried my hand at little brother, instead."

The anger in Suzy ratcheted up another level. An almost overwhelming sense of protectiveness toward James washed over her. It pushed out a question she'd wondered about since the night before.

"If you wanted to kill Gardner so badly, then why have a kid with him?"

Katrina scoffed. "It's hard to be a woman in my line of work, with my goals and ambitions, especially around here," she said. "When I first came to Riker, these rednecks with their simple ideas and lack of go-get-'em had the gall to look down on *me*. They didn't take me seriously. So I had to make them. It worked, mostly, but there were still some players out there I wanted to see quake at the very thought of me. So I decided I'd do some out-of-the-box thinking."

"You became partners with Gardner," Suzy guessed.

The woman nodded. "The idiot was lonely," she said, voice lacking any ounce of empathy. It made Suzy grit her teeth. "Convincing him that I loved him was too easy at first. Then I think he started to see the cracks. The poor guy had gone so soft that I knew if I got pregnant with his child, he'd stay by my side. A partnership that was good for business. Savvy, if I do say so myself."

Suzy was disgusted. "You tried to trap him," she bit out.

"It was nothing personal, just business."

Suzy couldn't think of a more personal thing than having a child with someone. Yet Katrina was acting like she'd never even entertained the idea that their kid was anything but a ploy to attach herself to Gardner.

"But Gardner saw through you," Suzy said. "He saw you for what you were and tried to leave."

Katrina's smirk started to slip. "He betrayed me," she hissed. "By stealing *my own child,* he made me look weak."

"That's the only reason you even want your son, isn't it?" Suzy realized the truth. "To prove to a bunch of criminals that you have your house in order. You don't even care about him, do you?"

Suzy was incensed. It seemed to feed Katrina.

"Aw, let me guess. You think all women should be mothers, and the fact that I could care less offends your maternal soul."

Suzy leaned as close to the woman as the chains would allow. A modicum of pleasure passed through her when she noticed the slight look of surprise on Katrina's face. It made the pain of moving worth it.

"*You* shouldn't be a mother," Suzy seethed. "And, in my book, you aren't."

Katrina glanced up at the chains. They rattled at Suzy's movement.

"Well, Suzy, tell me how you feel, why don't you," Katrina said with mock hurt. Suzy wasn't going to let the weight of the topic go. All she could think about was that baby boy growing up and knowing no love from the woman who had birthed him. If he were to stay with Katrina, he might not even have a chance at any type of love that was healthy and normal. The thought pushed Suzy close to her breaking point.

"Take me out of these chains and I'll show you instead," she threatened. "Or are you afraid you might break one of those manicured nails?"

As a woman who worked in law enforcement, Suzy had been underestimated by her fair share of people because she was a female. But she knew that a woman wasn't any less talented at her job just because she had pretty nails or liked wearing makeup.

Suzy also knew how to read someone. Knowing where their buttons were and when to push them was a part of the job she was constantly learning.

However, with Katrina, she'd just hit the jackpot.

The woman's lips narrowed; her nostrils flared. Dark eyes turned to slits.

Suzy couldn't help herself. "Looks like I hit a nerve," she said.

Katrina wasn't amused.

In record time she pulled something out of her pocket. Suzy didn't even have time to flinch away as Katrina drove the knife into her stomach.

But she had time to scream afterward.

"I think it's important to note the difference between our morals, Suzy," Katrina said at her ear. Suzy's vision blurred. "You might fight fair, but I *always* fight dirty."

IT WAS A bad case of déjà vu.

James stood at the back of the warehouse his brother had died in. He'd been back countless times since, trying to find some answers, but now everything felt different. That was because everything *was* different.

He'd lost a part of his family here. He wasn't going to let that happen again.

"No funny business, or Ryan here will break your knees," Grayton said, stretching tall and wide as soon as his shoes hit the dirt. The man named Ryan had been James's back-seat companion for the ride over. He had more weight and muscle than Grayton and James combined—not someone you'd bet against in a fight. James had spent the car ride trying to decide if the knife in the man's boot was the only weapon he had on him, or if he'd managed to hide a gun beneath his T-shirt. "Now, let's get this over with."

James let Grayton lead the way. So far, he'd decided to go along with the man's orders, let him think James wasn't going to resist. If he had been a smarter man, Grayton would have realized by now that James really only had one option.

Gather as much information as he could.

Then hit them all where it hurt.

It was a plan that was immediately put to the test. Two steps in and James was already seeing red.

Anger *and* blood.

Ryan grabbed James's shoulder and stopped

him from running forward as Grayton swung his gun to face him.

"Suzy!"

In the middle of the room, Suzy hung by her wrists. A knife was protruding from her stomach. Blood soaked through her shirt beneath it.

Katrina stood in front of her, smiling.

"And, just think, if you hadn't been such a heavy sleeper, then none of this would have happened," she said in greeting.

James was livid.

It didn't help matters when he saw Queso slumped against the wall in a similar fashion. If Chelsea, Justin and Cordelia were in the warehouse, at least they weren't hanging in this room.

"What did you do?" James roared, directing his rage toward Katrina. She gestured him and her men forward. Ryan's strength and Grayton's guns were the only things standing in the way of James unleashing his fury.

Katrina waved her hand in the air, dismissing his concern. "Don't worry, James," she said. "The chief deputy isn't dead. She's just unconscious." Her eyes trailed down to the knife. "Though I'm sure that can't be good. I suppose we should get down to business sooner rather than later."

Katrina snapped her fingers. From one of the warehouse's offices stepped another man, one James didn't recognize. Unlike Ryan, he was slight. Also unlike Ryan, he had a gun at his hip.

And Baby Gardner in his arms.

Chapter Twenty

"Let me make things simple," Katrina said, walking over to the two. She placed her finger on top of the boy's head. He started to fuss. "This is mine, and no matter what you do here today, he will stay mine. When I leave this ghastly building he will leave with me, and you will never see him again." She shrugged. "These are facts, not points of negotiation. However, here is what *is* up to you to decide."

She waved the man away just as Baby Gardner started to cry. James wanted to go to him, but knew the baby would probably be safer in the closed office than out there with them. Katrina moved until she was in front of James. Her smile never dropped.

"You can wire your fortune, using the computer in the lobby, to my untraceable account in the Caymans or I let Little Miss Authority here bleed out, dying near the same spot my dear Gardner did. Then I'll move on to the boy." She motioned to Queso. "And then I'll hunt Suzy's kid and gut him before it's your sister's turn." James's blood was boiling. "*Those* are your choices, Mr. Callahan."

"It's hardly a choice," he growled. His entire body was nearly vibrating with anger.

"That's the spirit. Grayton, make sure he does what he needs to," she ordered, waving her lackey to the front of the building. It was the only place that had power. Since James had bought the building, he had slowly started to work on converting it into something. He didn't know what yet, but in a weird way, working on the idea had made him feel closer to Gardner. Though now James wondered if he'd ever come back to the warehouse if they all managed to get out.

"Ryan, take our young friend in there with them," Katrina continued. "If Mr. Callahan gives either one of you any lip, start breaking the kid's bones. I don't care which ones."

James could barely keep it together as they walked out of the room, leaving Suzy behind. While he had no doubt that the vicious woman would do as she promised if he didn't cooperate, James also believed that it wouldn't matter if he did transfer the money without complaint. Katrina would kill the three of them and then disappear forever with his nephew. Which was why James was trying to shed his anger and focus as Queso was dragged into the room by his chains. He needed to make a move if they were all going to get out of the warehouse alive.

And not just any move. A smart one.

"Before you get any ideas, know that we made this really simple." Grayton pointed to the lone table. A laptop was on it, plugged in and open. A cell phone sat next to it. "You're going to put that on speaker while you call whoever is in charge of your finances to give you the account information. Then this is over."

Grayton waited for James to get in front of the screen. He kept the table between them, his gun at the ready.

"Without my phone I don't know his number," James said. It was the truth. "I'll need to look it up."

Grayton weighed that request for a moment then motioned to Ryan. "Watch him."

Ryan obliged and took up a spot at James's shoulder. He was glad the brute had stepped away from Queso. The boy was starting to stir.

"Don't worry about him," Grayton said. "Worry about the lady with the knife in her gut in the next room."

That got James going.

He pulled up a search window and went

about contacting his adviser, while being hyperaware of Queso's progress. A plan was starting to form. Maybe not the smartest one, but it was a plan, all the same.

And it required Queso's help.

"So I have to admit, after hearing a little background on you, I'm surprised you're taking orders so easily," James started. He kept up the appearance of searching around. "Grayton McKenzie, the errand boy for Gardner Todd's ex. Interesting that you traded your reputation for *that*. And who are we kidding? You're going to be her babysitter now, too. You've gone from being the top guy to cleaning diapers full of it."

Ryan surprised James by snorting behind him. Grayton was trying to play it cool, but anger flashed across his face at the sound. He stood up straighter and stared daggers at his brother in arms. It gave James the opening he needed. He looked over at Queso.

His eyes were open. And he was looking right at James.

"Shut up," Grayton said.

James took his hands off the laptop's keyboard and held them up in defense. "I'm just saying," he responded, hoping Queso was coherent enough to follow what he was about to try to convey. "If there's one thing I know about babies, it's that they can be a *distraction*."

The world around them seemed to slow. James felt a surge of adrenaline fill his veins. Every muscle tightened within him. All he needed was Queso to take the hint.

He didn't have to wait long. The boy's voice came out loud and clear.

"Padre's right about that."

It distracted Grayton, giving James an opening.

And he wasn't about to waste it.

Grabbing the underside of the table, James flipped it up. Before anything could settle, he bulldozed forward, using it as a battering ram. Together they connected with Grayton.

The man didn't have time to form his own attack. Instead, he was knocked off his feet and hit the ground hard. James kept the table on top of him, stomping down once before pivoting around. Every ounce of training and his workouts kicked into gear as James looked into the eyes of the charging bull that was Ryan. He was a big guy. A direct hit was going to hurt.

James decided he'd just not get hit.

Instead of readying a punch, he used the man's forward trajectory against him. James stepped to the side just enough that he could grab the front of Ryan's shirt before the man's beefy hands could land a blow. He took Ryan's momentum and employed it to his advantage. He swept the man's left foot out from under him while pulling down hard.

James pivoted once more, following the arc

until Ryan's face connected with the underside of the table. He groaned and tried to roll onto his back to get up, but James was faster. He kicked downward against the man's cheek.

It wasn't enough pressure to kill him, but enough to make his body go limp. A breath eased out of him as he slipped into unconsciousness.

"Padre, gun," Queso called.

James whipped around the table just as Grayton moved his arm forward. He was trying to grab the gun that he must have dropped while the table was being pushed into his body.

"I don't think so," James huffed, adrenaline still running high. He scooped the gun up before Grayton could even touch it. If half of his body hadn't been trapped beneath the table, which was now beneath Ryan, there was a good chance he would have been able to get at least one shot off before James could adapt.

James crouched down, level with the man's

eyes, and aimed the barrel of the gun at Grayton. When he spoke, he made sure his words were crystal clear.

"I'm going to give you something your boss wouldn't," he said. Grayton's eyes widened. "Mercy."

Relief flashed across the man's face. Still, James wasn't a chump. He used the own man's gun to knock him out.

Then James and Queso were the only conscious ones in the room.

He didn't want to let the streak of good luck die. Moving as fast as he could, James fished in Ryan's pockets until he had a key for Queso's chains and a cell phone.

"Where are Chelsea, Justin and Cordelia?" he asked as he went through the process of unlocking the clasps. There was blood on them where they had dug into Queso's skin.

"Shopping in Kipsy. It was just me and Suzy when crazy chick showed up."

James let out a small breath he'd been holding, relieved.

"Well, there's a piece of good news," he muttered.

The second the last clasp came undone, he handed Queso the cell phone.

"Call in backup and EMTs," he said. "Tell them an officer has been stabbed in the stomach and needs immediate care."

Queso rocked to his side, obviously trying to get up. "You need help now," he tried, wincing. He looked like someone had used him as a punching bag. "She had another guy with her at the house."

James shook his head, checked his gun and then pointed to the phone.

"Suzy needs you to make that call. *Now.*"

He didn't wait to see what the boy would say. Gun out, ready to pull the trigger when needed, James went back out into the main warehouse.

Neither Katrina nor her last lackey met him

there. Surely they'd heard the ruckus. James kept looking left and right, walking softly. No one jumped out or shot at him. That was good…but it also gave him a bad feeling.

Had Katrina already jumped ship? And with his nephew in tow?

James stopped at Suzy's side, eyes going straight to the knife.

This time it was he who had been distracted.

"Move and I shoot." Shame and anger set James's shoulders straight. "Drop the gun, slowly, or we shoot you both." Katrina's voice was calm. Steady. She meant what she said.

James didn't need to keep looking at Suzy— the beautiful woman he'd been lucky enough to fall asleep holding that morning—to know the risk wasn't worth her life.

His life, maybe, but not hers.

He did as he was told.

"Kick it away from you and turn around slowly," the lackey ordered.

Again, James followed the direction.

Katrina wasn't smiling anymore. "Do you know how a man like Lester got the drop on the infamous Gardner Todd?" she asked. Her voice was ice. "Gardner became sloppy. He didn't see a threat that was right in front of him. He was cocky. Just like you." She nodded to the office. The door was open. He'd been so transfixed by Suzy that he hadn't even heard them walk out.

"Some would call walking into the unknown courageous," he offered. "And one thing Gardner never lacked was courage."

"Courage has no place in this world," she snapped. "All it does is get people like you into a grave faster while pissing the rest of us off." Her stance changed. It hardened. She'd just come to a decision and was resolute about it. "I'm over it. And, just like Gardner, I'm over you."

A gunshot exploded through the warehouse. Followed by another. Then one more.

Baby Gardner started to cry.

James looked on, wide-eyed, as Katrina fell to the ground with a cry. Her lackey dropped next.

A fourth person moved farther inside the room.

It was Sully.

He looked rough, slouched and holding his side with one hand and his gun in the other, but he was still standing.

James couldn't claim the same.

Sully cursed something wicked and called out to him. But it was too late.

James clutched the bullet wound in his stomach and stumbled to the ground. The last thing he saw before the world got dark was the face of a beautiful woman.

Chapter Twenty-One

Suzy smelled the cake before she ever saw her mother.

Cordelia peeked around the door mere seconds before walking in uninvited, cake tin in hand.

"I brought cake," she whispered, holding the tin up as if Suzy hadn't seen it. "He said pound cake was his favorite. So here I am!"

Suzy put her finger to her lips, and the older woman's eyes widened. They both glanced at the hospital bed in the space between them. James was asleep. He had been since that morning. The night before, he'd woken up for the first time since surgery. But then Suzy had been asleep, riding her own wave of pain medications. The same thing had happened that morning. It felt like they were star-crossed lovers, just waiting for word when the other one was conscious.

Finally Suzy had given up and decided to park herself on the couch in his room. If Katrina's knife hadn't managed to miss her major organs, Suzy knew it would be a different story. Yet the tides had turned and she was the one in the hospital room who was in the better condition. Though the nurses were keeping an eye out on her. If she moved around too much she would be banished back to her own room.

She wanted to thank James for what he'd done.

She also just wanted to know he was okay.

The doctors might have already given him two thumbs up after his surgery, but she needed more proof. And she desperately wanted to see the man smile.

"Where's Chelsea?" her mother asked, putting the cake tin on the table that already held a myriad of flowers. All were from residents of Bates Hill. Once word had gotten out that their beloved millionaire was in the hospital, the floral population in the private wing had grown exponentially. "Did I miss her on the way up here?"

The older woman went to Suzy's legs, picked them up carefully and then sat beneath them. She readjusted the blanket so it was over both of them. Very much a woman who meant to stay for the long haul.

It warmed Suzy's heart.

"They finally cleared Queso to leave, so Chelsea took him back to the estate," she answered. "I suggested she look after him for a few hours, and I said I'd call her if James decided to stop auditioning for Sleeping Beauty."

The older woman smiled. She looked over at James. "Maybe he just needs to be kissed by his one true love," she suggested.

While Suzy might have warned her mother

off the week before, flustered by the sugges-
tion and even opposed to it, now she found
herself smiling.

"I heard his friend is doing better now," her
mother said, apparently deciding not to push
the topic of kissing James Callahan. Though
Suzy knew that would probably only last until
both were discharged from the hospital.

"Douglas? Yeah, thank goodness Queso
sent first responders to the estate, too, when
he made the call for backup. The doctor said
Douglas might not have made it another hour,
otherwise."

The older woman nodded and then patted
Suzy's leg. "It's been one heck of a year," she
pointed out. "One too many hospital trips for
my liking."

Suzy tried to reach out to touch her mother's
hand, but the stitches across her knife wound
pulled. She lowered herself back down. Her
mother frowned. "One too many scars on my
baby girl."

"Mom, didn't you hear? Guys dig scars. Or, wait, is that just chicks?"

It took a moment, but her mother laughed. "Oh, Suzy Q, I do think you're the best thing I've done in my life." Her expression softened. "I'm sure wherever your daddy is right now, he's so proud of you."

The warmth in Suzy's heart grew in size. While they often drove each other crazy, at the end of the day, their love was strong.

Being reminded of that did Suzy some good. She surprised her mother by being completely honest, no humor attached. "Billy told me that Daddy would have liked James. I believe him, too. Even if he hadn't taken a bullet for me, I think he's one of the best people I've ever met or will meet."

Her mother's smile was back in force. "I agree." There was a glint in the older woman's eye, a look that told Suzy her mother had, indeed, picked up on the fact that Suzy and James had gotten close. In more ways than one. "He's got a big heart. But..."

Suzy felt her eyebrows rise. While she'd been more than ready to criticize James the week before, now she'd gotten to know him. Gotten to know his family. Understood that he would always do his best to help people, especially those closest to him. He was a compassionate man, and that, above all else, had made her fall in love with him.

Which was definitely something she hoped to explore with him when he was out of recovery.

So, what strike could her mother have against him? "But?" she repeated.

Her mother let out a long, low sigh. "But when you two need a babysitter, please look somewhere else, because, honey, I already did my time with you and Justin, and goodness knows I need all the help I can get when it comes to beauty sleep."

Suzy wanted to laugh but knew the movement would upset her stitches and be more than painful. Instead she smiled. Her mother, tough as nails, had a habit of becoming cranky if her eight hours weren't met.

"Mom, Mara has been babysitting the last two days. Not you," Suzy reminded her. "You and Justin weren't even in the same house with them!"

Her mother shrugged. "I'm just letting you know that, while I don't mind helping out every now and then, you two are young enough to take on the task of trying to get that baby boy on a normal sleep schedule."

Suzy rolled her eyes and glanced at James. He was looking right back, smiling.

The worry that had clenched itself around her heart like a vise finally loosened.

"Is it just the pain meds or do I smell cake?" he asked.

And just like that, Suzy felt like she could fully breathe again.

TWO WEEKS LATER, James was sitting on his back patio, enjoying the weather and holding his nephew, when Hank approached him. Hank didn't wait for an invitation and took a seat in what James was hoping would be Suzy's chair when she arrived for lunch. He had two envelopes in his hand.

"I hear you took out Grayton McKenzie with a table," he said in greeting. "I have to say I'm sorry I missed that. I guess your brother wasn't the only one who could think on his feet."

James smiled. He considered it a compliment. "I hear you took out two men with your bare hands at Suzy's house, not to mention the men you fought off at The Tavern," he pointed out. "Maybe we're all a little like Gardner at the end of the day."

Hank chuckled. The baby in James's arms wiggled but didn't wake. Hank looked down at the boy. The sleeping baby seemed to sober him.

"While I'd really get a kick out of you describing handing Grayton his backside in detail, I got my lady in the car and some business to finish before we leave." He took the first envelope and set it down on the patio table at James's side. "This is for you from me. Well, from your brother, really. It's the deed to the bar. It's yours now."

James couldn't hide his surprise. "The Tavern? I can't take your bar."

Hank grinned. "Never was really mine," he said. "When I first met Gardner I was pretty down on my luck. I had problems on problems, and nowhere and no one to turn to but the bottle. I find myself at an old bar, wasted and alone, when this guy takes a seat on the stool next to me and just starts talking. At first I didn't know what he was yammering on about. He opened with a joke about the weather, but he kept going, and then I started yammering, too. The next thing I knew, I was a regular and Gardner was a friend.

"Then, soon after that, he offered me a job. Said I had good character and he needed someone like that to take over the bar and run things." He shrugged. "I thought the man was crazy for just giving it to me, but I took the job with pride. Gardner floated around after that, but when he was in town he'd come in. Eventually he started opening up a bit, talking about how he wished his brother could see the place. Said you two used to talk about owning a bar when you were younger."

James smiled. Gardner had named the bar The Tavern because they had picked it out when they were boys.

Hank didn't miss the smile. "Anyways, since I can never repay Gardner for what he did, I thought I'd at least do something he never could." He motioned to the envelope again. "I think he thought one day he'd finally show the place to you, so it only seems fitting."

James kept his smile but shook his head. "I appreciate it, I really do, but I can't take your bar. I'll just come in and drink at it, instead."

This time Hank was the one who shook his head.

"Because of it and Gardner, me and my lady

are good on money. Plus, we're feeling restless. Might hop on up to North Carolina to see
some of her kin, or just jump a plane to Ha-
waii for a few weeks." He shrugged. "I don't
need the bar anymore. And, really, I think I
was always just holding on to it for you. All
I ask is that you keep Rudy on. He's a good
guy. Deal?"

James didn't have to think long. "Deal," he
agreed.

"Good." Hank put the second envelope on
the table. Unlike the other one, it had the letter *J* handwritten on its front. It was also much
thicker. James sat straighter. "I can't speak for
Gardner on most things, but what I can say is
this. He loved that kid in your arms, and he
loved you and your sister something fierce. In
that envelope is proof of both. But that's something you should read on your own. I won't
spoil it."

Hank stood. He held his hand out. James
shook it.

"And now it's time for me to go. You take care of yourself and that little boy."

James stood, moving the sleeping child to his other arm. The baby stirred, but again didn't wake.

"You too, Hank. I can't thank you enough for everything you did."

The man smirked. "Buy me a drink whenever I'm back in town and we'll be square," he said.

James laughed. "I guess now I know just the place."

Hank didn't linger. He walked around the side of the house and was gone. A few seconds later the back door opened.

"Hey, Padre, was that Hank?"

James turned to see Queso walking over. Like James and Suzy, he'd had to be hospitalized after the warehouse. Or, more accurately, after what had happened at the estate. According to Suzy, Queso had done everything in his power to try to protect her and the baby. Just as he'd tried to help Chelsea and James when Katrina had first broken in. James was still trying to find a way to repay him for both. He figured giving the young man a place to stay for a while was the least he could do. And, he had to admit, he was happy that the boy had agreed.

Sully had come in and helped save the day, shooting both Katrina and her henchman before either could finish the job on him or kill Suzy. When Sully had gone to get the information that James had asked for on Gardner after they'd met in the freezer, Sully had been ambushed by Katrina. She'd nearly killed him. He, however, had decided to only wound her and not end her life when the opportunity arose.

"I want her to sit in a prison cell, letting everyone know that Sully the Butcher doesn't stand for anything she did," he'd told James in the hospital. At the time, James had made his own decision not to mention that a lot of the anger Sully was feeling had to do with the beating Katrina's men had given Queso. Sully might pretend to be tough, but there was undoubtedly a soft spot there for the boy.

Which made his insistence that Queso leave his organization surprising. Or maybe not.

"I don't think that kid ever believed in what we do," he'd said. "I think he just needed to belong somewhere."

Now that somewhere included being with James, Chelsea, Baby Gardner, Justin, Cordelia and Suzy. Since they'd been released from the hospital, they'd all seen a lot of one another.

"It sure was," James answered, scooping up the envelope with The Tavern's deed in it. "Too bad you're not twenty-one yet. Because apparently, Queso, we now own a bar."

The boy looked confused but didn't have time to ask for an explanation. Baby Gardner started to fuss.

"Chelsea sent me out here to get him," he said. "It's time for his food."

James passed the baby over with a laugh and then looked at the second envelope on the table.

"You two head in," he said. "I need to read something first."

Queso didn't question him. However, he did pause in the doorway. "Oh, and, Padre? You can call me by my real name. It's Jensen."

Then the boy was in the kitchen, the door shut behind him. James couldn't help but smile wide.

"Deal," he said to himself, sitting back down. He opened the envelope, trying to ready himself for what he was about to find.

It was a fool's errand.

Gardner had managed to fill the envelope with three things. The first was an official birth certificate. His son had been born in Birmingham, and his name was Adam. James took a minute to let that sink in. An unexpected weight lifted as he finally knew the name his brother had given his only son.

The second thing was a letter to Adam with a note to read it when he was eighteen. James made the decision not to open it himself.

The third thing was the one that consumed James. It was a letter to him, typed in small font over the front and back and dated a week before Gardner died. It was long and heart-felt, and for the first time James had a clearer picture of his brother's last ten years. Gardner told stories about his life, along with hopes he had for the future, and fears and regrets he had from the past. He apologized for who he had become, but said he was proud of who James had turned into. And then he told James what he had already guessed. Once Gardner became a father, he'd planned to leave his criminal life to do right by his kid.

This was hard to process all at once for James. He knew he'd spend years going over the letter, reading it when he missed his big brother, but there was one line that James would never forget.

Just remember, kid, life is chaos, but that never has to be a bad thing.

As he put the letter back in the envelope, the sound of laughter came through the back door. James watched as a conga line of people marched out with food on their plates. Chelsea had Adam and both were giggling at something while Jensen balanced their plates. Justin and Cordelia were right behind them, having their own conversation, which meant the woman he'd seen every day since the hospital was not far behind.

Two seconds later he was staring at that beautiful face, grin and all. She dropped her plate off at the patio table and walked over with purpose. That purpose included a kiss against his lips and a laugh. She eyed the envelopes and then his face, picking up on the emotions he'd just flown through at receiving each, he had no doubt. James liked to believe he was hard to read but was finding there was one woman who had no problem doing exactly that.

She dropped into the chair next to him and leaned over, expression turning serious.

"You know, I realized today that you haven't had an empty house in weeks. Just say the word and me and mine could stay clear for a few days if you need a break. Or longer. It's up to you."

Even though she was offering, James could see the hesitation behind it. She didn't like the idea of them spending time apart.

Neither did he.

He felt a smile as genuine as they came pull up the corners of his lips.

"Oh, no you don't, Suzanne Simmons. You're not getting off that easy." He motioned to his stomach. "I took a bullet for you, so, by my calculation, I think you owe me at the very least several years of companionship." Suzy started to mimic his smile. He reached out and took her hand. "Plus, I'm pretty sure I'm the one that got you into trouble with the sheriff's wife over a dress I helped ruin?"

Suzy tossed her head back and laughed. James didn't know what he would do in a world where he couldn't hear that sound every day.

"I guess you do owe me, then," she decided. "And it was such a nice dress. Definitely worth a few years of trying to make it up to me. Though maybe you can start trying... Say, tonight after everyone goes to bed?"

There was a mischievousness in her eyes that excited James to no end. He pulled her to him and gave her another kiss.

"Ew, gross," Justin called from behind them.

"I second that," Jensen added.

"I think it's adorable," Chelsea tacked on.

"I second that," Cordelia said.

Suzy broke the kiss and sighed. She was still smiling.

"This is what we're signing up for, you know? One big, messy family. It'll be chaos."

James didn't miss a beat.

"But the best kind."

* * * * *